Organ Music
by French Masters

ORGAN MUSIC BY FRENCH MASTERS

13 WORKS BY GOUNOD, SAINT-SAËNS, CHAUSSON, SATIE AND OTHERS

SELECTED AND WITH AN INTRODUCTION BY
ROLLIN SMITH

DOVER PUBLICATIONS, INC.
Mineola, New York

Copyright

Copyright © 2004 by Dover Publications, Inc.
All rights reserved.

Bibliographical Note

This Dover edition, first published in 2004, is a new compilation of works originally published separately. The introductory notes have been specially prepared by Rollin Smith for this edition, and some works have been newly engraved.

International Standard Book Number: 0-486-43584-9

Manufactured in the United States of America
Dover Publications, Inc., 31 East 2nd Street, Mineola, N.Y. 11501

CONTENTS

BOËLY, Alexandre-P.-F.	Style Moderne, Op. 43, No. 8	2
GOUNOD, Charles	Marche Solennelle	6
SAINT-SAËNS, Camille	Fantaisie in E-flat	12
GIGOUT, Eugène	Grand Chœur dialogué	21
GUILMANT, Alexandre	Marche sur un Thème de Hændel, Op. 15, No. 2	28
MASSENET, Jules	Prélude en Ut Majeur	36
CHAUSSON, Ernest	Les Vêpres des Vierges, Op. 31	
	I. Hæc est virgo Sapiens et una	38
	II. Hæc est virgo Sapiens, quam Dominus	38
	III. Hæ est quæ nescivit	39
	IV. Veni electa mea	39
	V. Ista est speciosa	39
	VI. Veni sponsa Christi	40
	VII. Prudentes Virgines	42
	VIII. Veni sponsa Christi	47
	AUTRES ANTIENNES BRÈVES POUR LE MAGNIFICAT	
	I. [Modéré]	51
	II. [Sans lenteur]	52
	III. [Mouv^t. de Choral]	53
BOËLLMANN, Léon	Suite Gothique, Op. 25	
	I. Introduction – Choral	54
	II. Menuet gothique	56
	III. Prière à Notre-Dame	61
	IV. Toccata	65
PIERNÉ, Gabriel	Trois Pièces, Op. 29	
	I. Prélude	75
	II. Cantilène	80
	III. Scherzando de Concert	84
SATIE, Erik	Messe des Pauvres	
	I. [Kyrie eleison]	94
	II. Dixit domine	98
	III. Prière des Orgues	99
	IV. Commune qui mundi nefas	101
	V. Chant Ecclésiastique	102
	VI. Prière pour les voyageurs et les marins en danger de mort, à la très bonne et très august Vierge Marie, mère de Jésus.	102
	VII. Prière pour le salut de mon âme	103
ROGER-DUCASSE, Jean	Pastorale	104
IBERT, Jacques	Trois Pièces	
	I. Pièce solennelle	118
	II. Musette	124
	III. Fugue	129
HONEGGER, Arthur	Two Pieces	
	I. Fugue	135
	II. Choral	138

NOTES ON THE MUSIC

LÉON BOËLLMANN
SUITE GOTHIQUE, Op. 25

Born in Alsace, Léon Boëllmann studied at the École Niedermeyer in Paris, won first prize in all his subjects and, in 1881, at the age of nineteen, was appointed *organiste de chœur,* or choir accompanist, at the Church of Saint-Vincent-de-Paul. He succeeded to the post of *organiste titulaire* in 1896, but died the following year at the age of thirty-five.

Boëllmann left sixty-eight published works, but his *Variations symphoniques* for cello and orchestra, first played at the Concerts Lamoureaux in 1892, and the *Suite gothique* for organ, have become standards in their respective repertoires. The latter was published in 1895 and dedicated to the American organist William C. Carl. It has remained a favorite with organists for over a century owing as much to its flowing, charming melodies, as to its colorful harmony, expressive counterpoint, and delightful modulations.

ALEXANDRE-PIERRE-FRANÇOIS BOËLY
STYLE MODERNE, Op. 43, No. 8

Boëly, remembered as "The French Bach," was the first organist in Paris to have a pedalboard with a compass of over two octaves on which he could play the music of Bach. It was said in the middle of the nineteenth century that Boëly was one of two or three French organists capable of playing a fugue correctly.

Slow movements, which Boëly called *Style Moderne,* are his single greatest contribution to organ literature. It is in these that he foreshadows the emotionally-charged slow movements of Franck and Vierne. Indeed, this Larghetto in C-sharp minor may well have inspired César Franck's *Prière* in the same key: both have the same atmosphere and harmonies. In calling these pieces "style moderne," Boëly was not trying to imitate earlier styles, as he often did in his organ music, but was indeed writing in his own style. This excerpt is from a collection of twelve pieces published posthumously in 1860.

ERNEST CHAUSSON
LES VÊPRES DES VIERGES, Op. 31

Best known for his *Poème* for violin and orchestra, Ernest Chausson was possessed of independent means and wrote relatively little music. His organ music comprises this set of *versets,* or organ interludes, to be played as alternate verses to those sung by the choir. The set includes five antiphons for the psalms sung at Vespers, three antiphons for the Magnificat, and three other brief antiphons for the Magnificat. Opus 31 was composed during November and December 1897 while Chausson was on vacation with his family in Fiesole, near Florence, Italy. It was published in 1898, and played for the first time by Charles Tournemire during a concert at the Schola Cantorum on March 3, 1901.

EUGÈNE GIGOUT
GRAND CHŒUR DIALOGUÉ

Eugène Gigout was organist of the Parisian Church of Saint-Augustin from 1863 until his death in 1925—a total of sixty-two years. In 1911 he succeeded Alexandre Guilmant as professor of organ at the Paris Conservatoire and numbered Maurice Duruflé and André Fleury among his students. No less a critic than Camille Saint-Saëns regarded Gigout as the greatest organist he had ever known—both technically and as a marvelous improviser. The *Grand Chœur dialogué,* composed around 1881, is Gigout's most famous piece and exploits the traditional position of the two organs in French churches: the small *orgue de chœur* in the front near the altar for accompanying the choir and the large *grand orgue* in the rear gallery over the entrance. The sound of the two instruments playing antiphonally creates a dramatic effect.

CHARLES GOUNOD
MARCHE SOLENNELLE

The manuscript of this work is dated May 22, 1889. It is dedicated to Lucie Palicot, a virtuoso on the pédalier, or pedal piano, who, incidentally, toured the United States in the fall of 1893. Gounod, wishing to "flatter her talent," as a biographer subtly expressed it, composed several pieces for the pédalier, with and without orchestra. His dedication to Mlle Palicot was tactfully left off the posthumously published score by his family. On the first page of the three-stave version for Grand Orgue the words "ou Piano-Pédalier" are printed in small letters, indicating that the *Marche Solennelle* was intended for the pédalier as much as for the organ.

ALEXANDRE GUILMANT
MARCHE SUR UN THÈME DE HÆNDEL, Op. 15, No. 2

At the turn of the twentieth century, Félix-Alexandre Guilmant was famous not only as an organ virtuoso (he visited nearly all the countries of Europe and made three voyages to the United States) but as an improviser, teacher, composer, and music editor. From 1896 until his death in 1911 he was professor of organ at the Paris Conservatoire (numbering Marcel Dupré, Joseph Bonnet, and Nadia Boulanger among his students) as well as at the Schola Cantorum, of which he was a founder.

This *Marche* was composed on October 22, 1861, while Guilmant was organist of the Church of Saint-Nicolas in his home town of Boulogne-sur-Mer, ten years before he went to Paris as organist of La Trinité. While the first four notes are also those of the chorus, "Lift up your heads, O ye gates," from Handel's *Messiah,* it is curious that the *Marche* bears more similarities with Giuseppe Giordani's song, "Caro mio ben,"—eight notes, an identical bass line, and almost the same harmony.

viii

ARTHUR HONEGGER
TWO PIECES

Born in Le Havre of Swiss parents, Honegger studied at the Paris Conservatoire with André Gédalge and Charles-Marie Widor and later with Vincent d'Indy. He was a member of the group of young French composers—Milhaud, Poulenc, Auric, Durey, and Tailleferre—that was dubbed "Les Six" in 1920.

Honegger was not an organist and was confused about the range of the pedalboard: he consistently wrote the pedal part of the *Fugue in C-sharp Minor* (though, curiously, not the *Choral*) an octave higher than he intended it to sound. Lynnwood Farnam (1885–1930) rescored the work and wrote much of the pedal part an octave lower.

The *Choral,* dated September 1917, was written while Honegger was still studying with Widor. It is dedicated to Andrée Vaurabourg, a pianist who frequently played his works, whom he married in 1926.

JACQUES IBERT
TROIS PIÈCES

Jacques Ibert won the Prix de Rome in 1919 and became one of France's more distinguished composers. His style is derived from the impressionists but shaped by the Satie-influenced post–First World War French school. He wrote little for the organ, his main contribution being these *Three Pieces* published in 1920.

JULES MASSENET
PRÉLUDE EN UT MAJEUR

There is no record at the Paris Conservatoire of Jules Massenet having studied organ, though he did win first prizes in piano and fugue and, in 1863, the Prix de Rome. Chiefly known as the composer of some twenty-seven operas, *Manon* being considered his masterpiece, he composed little sacred music. This *Prelude in C Major* is his only organ work and was published in 1911, during the last year of his life.

GABRIEL PIERNÉ
TROIS PIÈCES

Gabriel Pierné studied at the Paris Conservatoire with César Franck and Jules Massenet. At the age of nineteen he won the Prix de Rome and when he returned to Paris he succeeded Franck as organist a Sainte-Clotilde, remaining there until 1896. In 1903 he was appointed assistant conductor to Édouard Colonne and in 1910 his successor. A conformist, Pierné was not concerned with experimentation but only with the projection of poetic beauty and sensitive moods in an elegant style.

JEAN ROGER-DUCASSE
PASTORALE

Written in 1909, this *Pastorale* was dedicated to Nadia Boulanger and premiered on April 20, 1910, by Alexandre Guilmant. The great American organist Lynnwood Farnam wrote the following program note:

> This remarkable composition is founded upon a single theme of a pastoral nature. The original intention of the composer was to write a simple piece of but three or four pages, but at the solicitation of friends who suggested a further development he achieved a great masterpiece of organ literature, his only published work for the instrument. Its charm lies in its delicate fancy, graceful sallies for flute stops, scintillating scherzo movement, and the reverie following the stormy climax. In addition to this it is a rare example of the felicitous and inspired use of varied contrapuntal resources and calls for organ-registration effects of exceptional color and contrast.

CAMILLE SAINT-SAËNS
FANTAISIE IN E-FLAT

Saint-Saëns won a First Prize in organ at the Paris Conservatoire in 1851, and two years later, at the age of seventeen, was appointed organist of the Church of Saint-Merry. Four years later the much-repaired and restored seventeenth-century organ was rebuilt by Aristide Cavaillé-Coll. Saint-Saëns composed this *Fantaisie,* his first published organ work, in two days, May 12 and 13, 1857, and played it for the first time at the inauguration of the organ on December 3.

This *Fantaisie* is a light-hearted virtuoso piece by a composer who thought it was "fun" to play the organ. The *Con moto* begins with alternating chords on three contrasting keyboards and is followed by an *Allegro di molto e con fuoco* in which, amid scale passages and harmonic progressions, a short one-page fugue is inserted; it ends with an ascending octave run and a *sforzando* series of chords.

ERIK SATIE
MESSE DES PAUVRES

In his early twenties Erik Satie immersed himself in the self-conscious medievalism of the Rosicrucian sect and the study of plainsong. The 1895 *Messe des pauvres* for optional voices and organ is a result of those studies. Wilfred Mellers, in the fifth edition of Grove's Dictionary, wrote that in the various movements

> curiously unrelated chromatic harmonies accompany melodies which are non-metrical and fluid in rhythm; the plainsong and organum technique divests the sophisticated harmonies of any dramatic significance. One imagines that plainsong appealed to Satie not for its mystical implications, but precisely because of its aloofness and impersonality.

ROLLIN SMITH

Organ Music
by French Masters

Dediée à son ami Georges Schmitt

FANTAISIE IN E-FLAT

CAMILLE SAINT-SAËNS
1835–1921

16

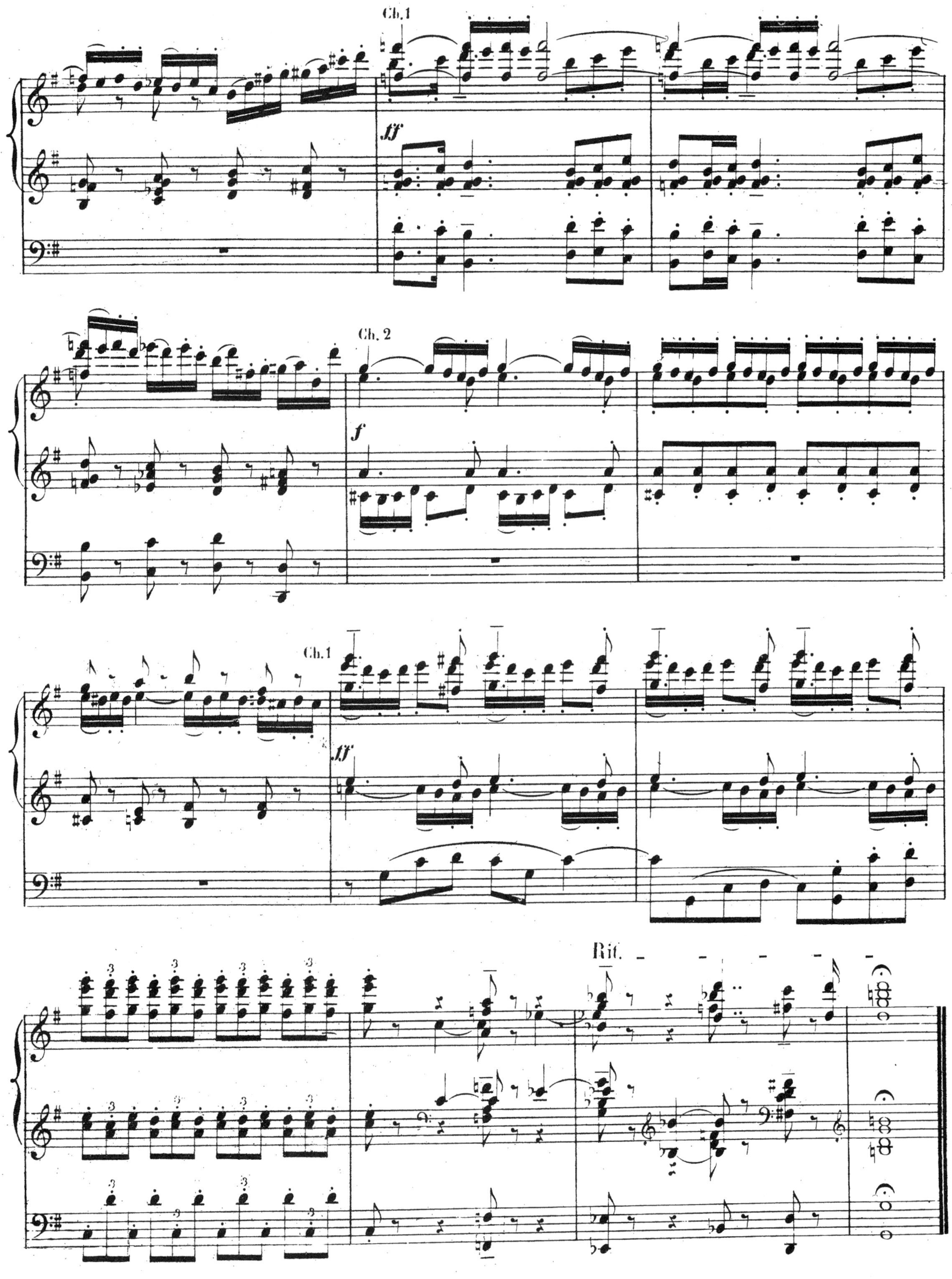
Ch. 1
ff
Ch. 2
f
Ch. 1
ff
Rit.

Hommage à THALBERG

MARCHE

SUR UN THÈME DE HÆNDEL

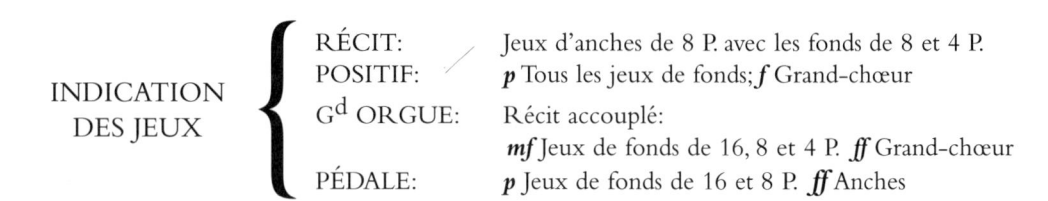

Op. 15, No. 2

INDICATION
DES JEUX

RÉCIT: Jeux d'anches de 8 P. avec les fonds de 8 et 4 P.
POSITIF: *p* Tous les jeux de fonds; *f* Grand-chœur
Gᵈ ORGUE: Récit accouplé:
mf Jeux de fonds de 16, 8 et 4 P. *ff* Grand-chœur
PÉDALE: *p* Jeux de fonds de 16 et 8 P. *ff* Anches

ALEXANDRE GUILMANT
1837–1911

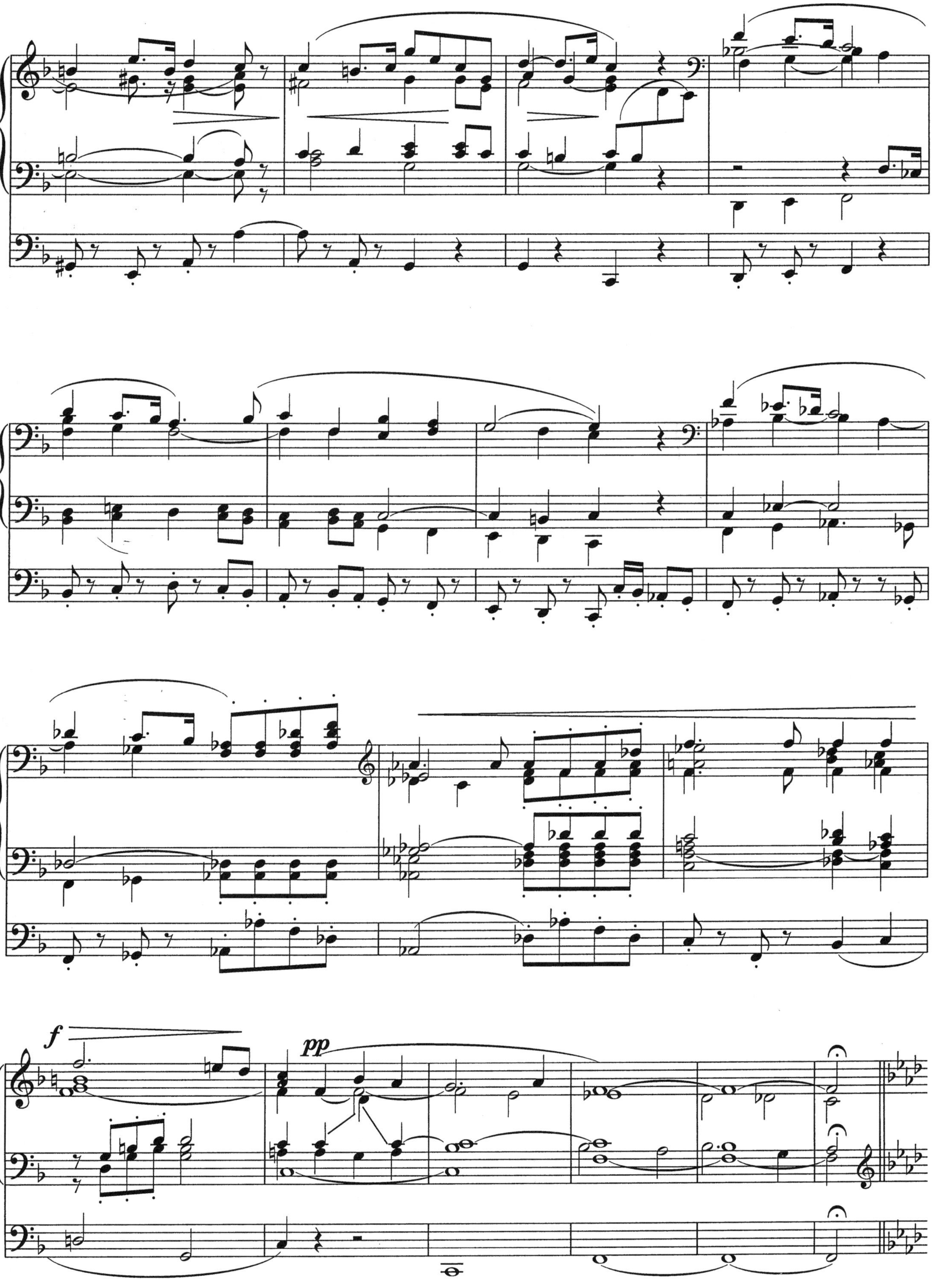

f
pp

Più mosso ♩ = 80
mf Grand-Orgue (Récit fermé)
ajoutez les jeux de fonds de 4 P. et la Tirasse.

31

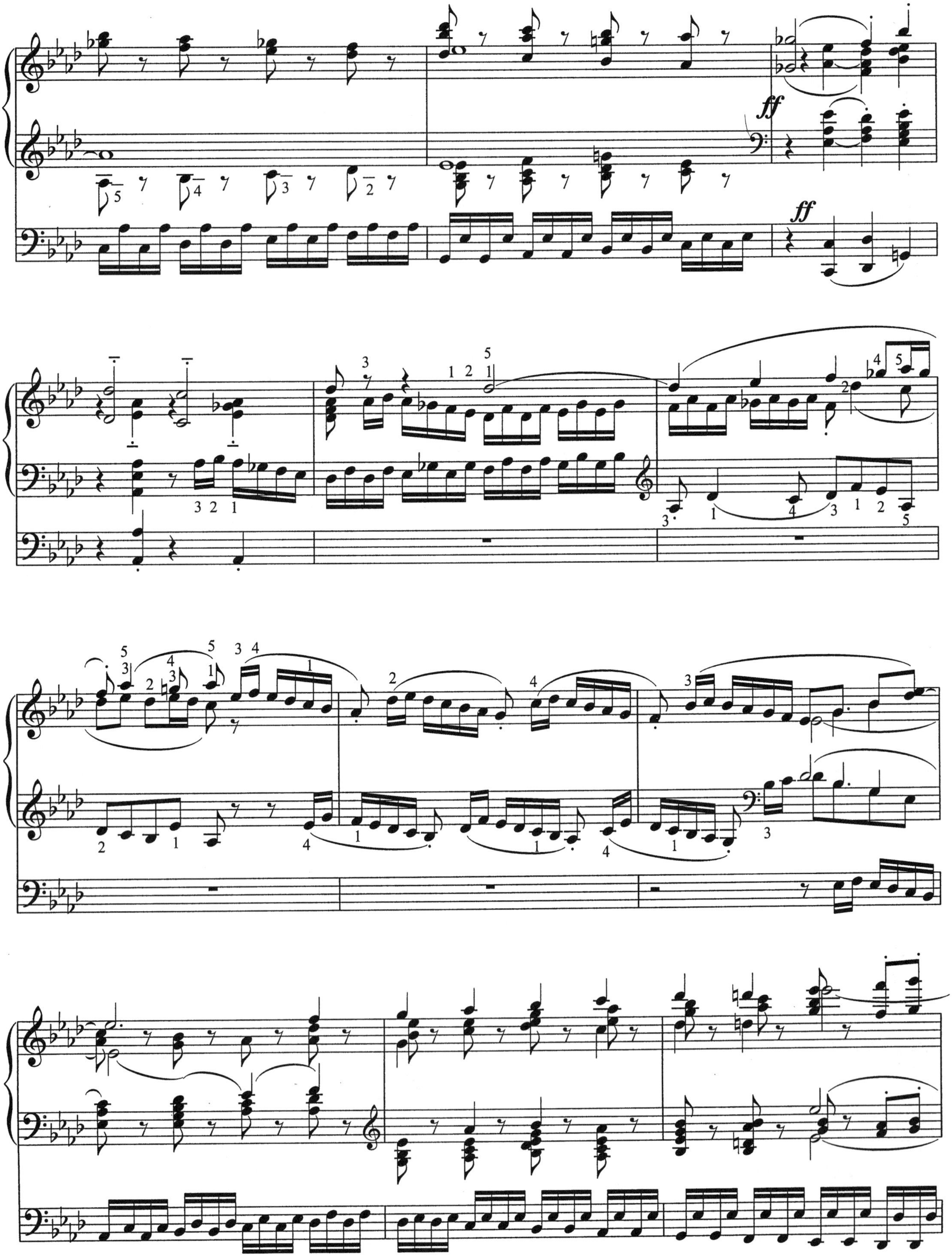
ff
ff

Positif
Récit
2
4
m.d.
Récit
Récit
Positif
Récit
m.d.
Récit
Positif
Récit
Récit
Positif
Récit
m.d.
Positif
Récit
cresc.
Positif
3 2 1

Récit ouvert
cresc.
accelerando poco
Grand-Orgue mf 3 2 1
G.-O.
Positif f accouplé au Gd.-O.
rit.
molto rall.
1º tempo maestoso
fff tutta la forza

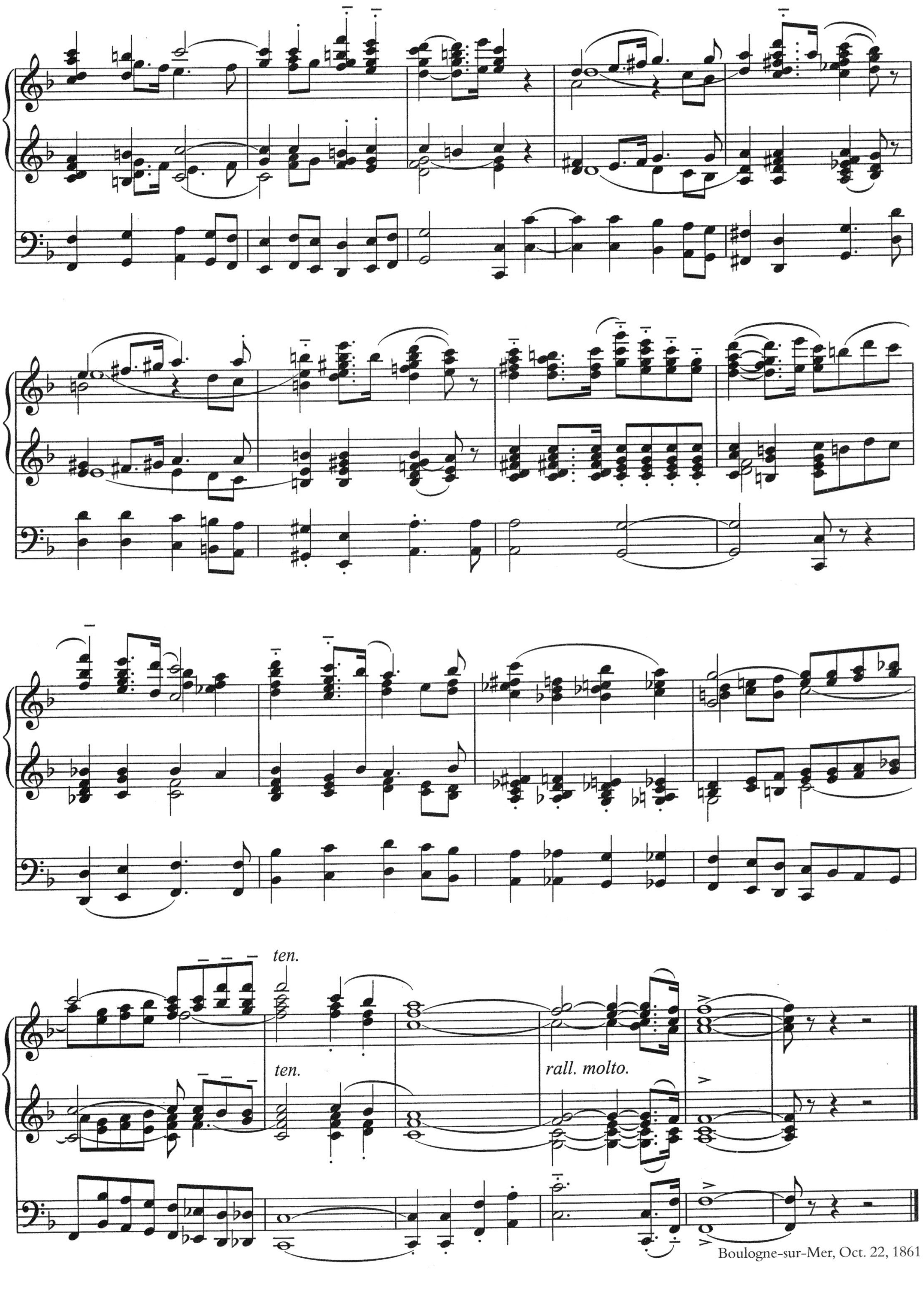

Boulogne-sur-Mer, Oct. 22, 1861

PRÉLUDE EN UT MAJEUR

à Monsieur l'Abbé LOUIS
Organiste au Collège St-Joseph à Poitiers

J. MASSENET
1842-1912

Très modéré

GRAND-ORGUE

PÉDALES

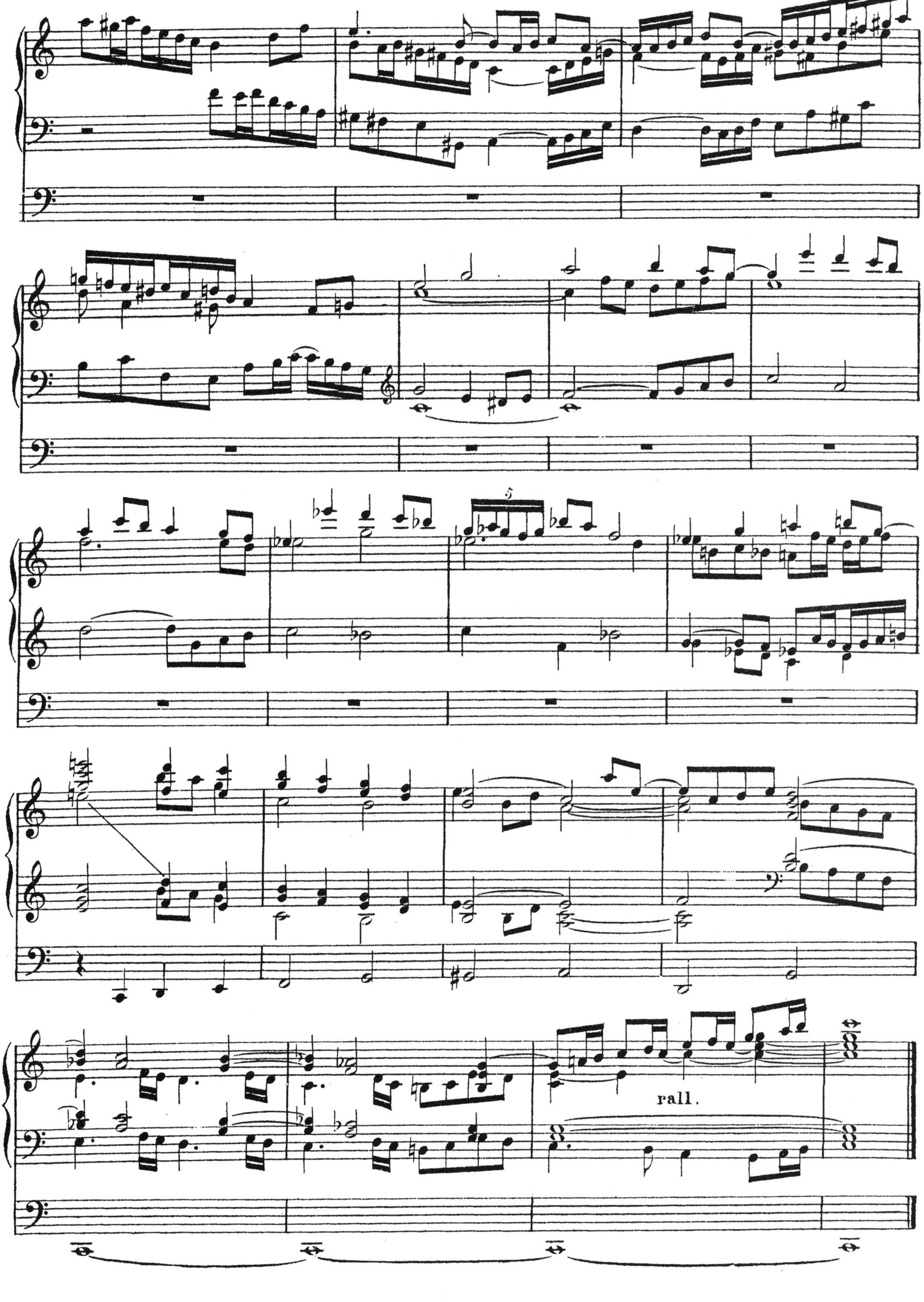
rall.

A Mademoiselle ANNIE CHAUSSON

LES VÊPRES DES VIERGES

Op. 31

ERNEST CHAUSSON
1855–1899

Hæc est virgo Sapiens et una
Antienne du 1er Mode.

Hæc est quæ nescivit

Antienne du 3e Mode.

à Magnificat: Veni sponsa Christi
Antienne du 8.e Mode.

VI Sans lenteur.

✳ Si l'on veut écourter ces Antiennes, l'organiste trouvera le Cadence nécessaire aux ✳ placés au cours d'elles.

VII. Prudentes Virgines
Antienne du 4e Mode.

Modéré.

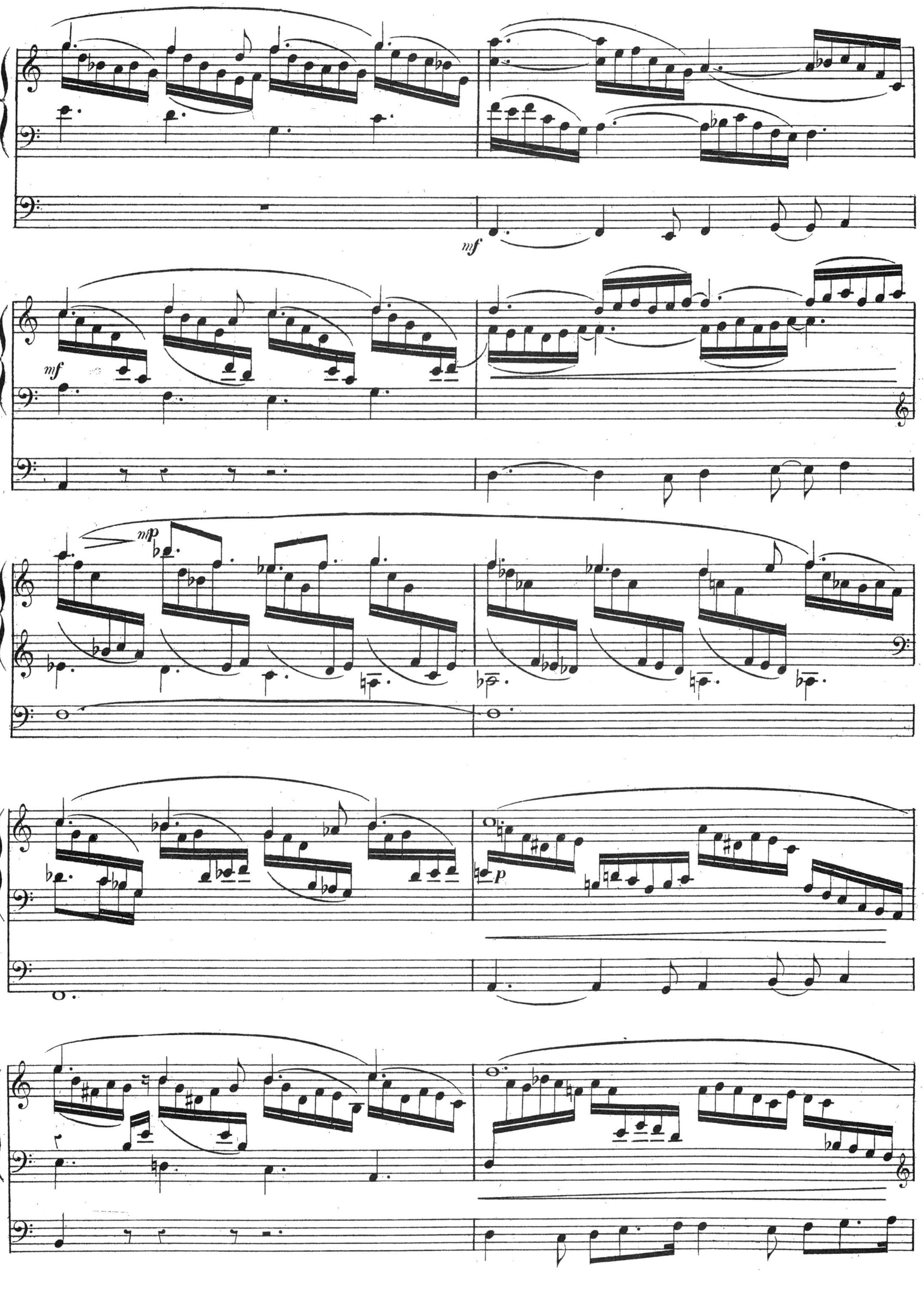
mf
mf
mp
p

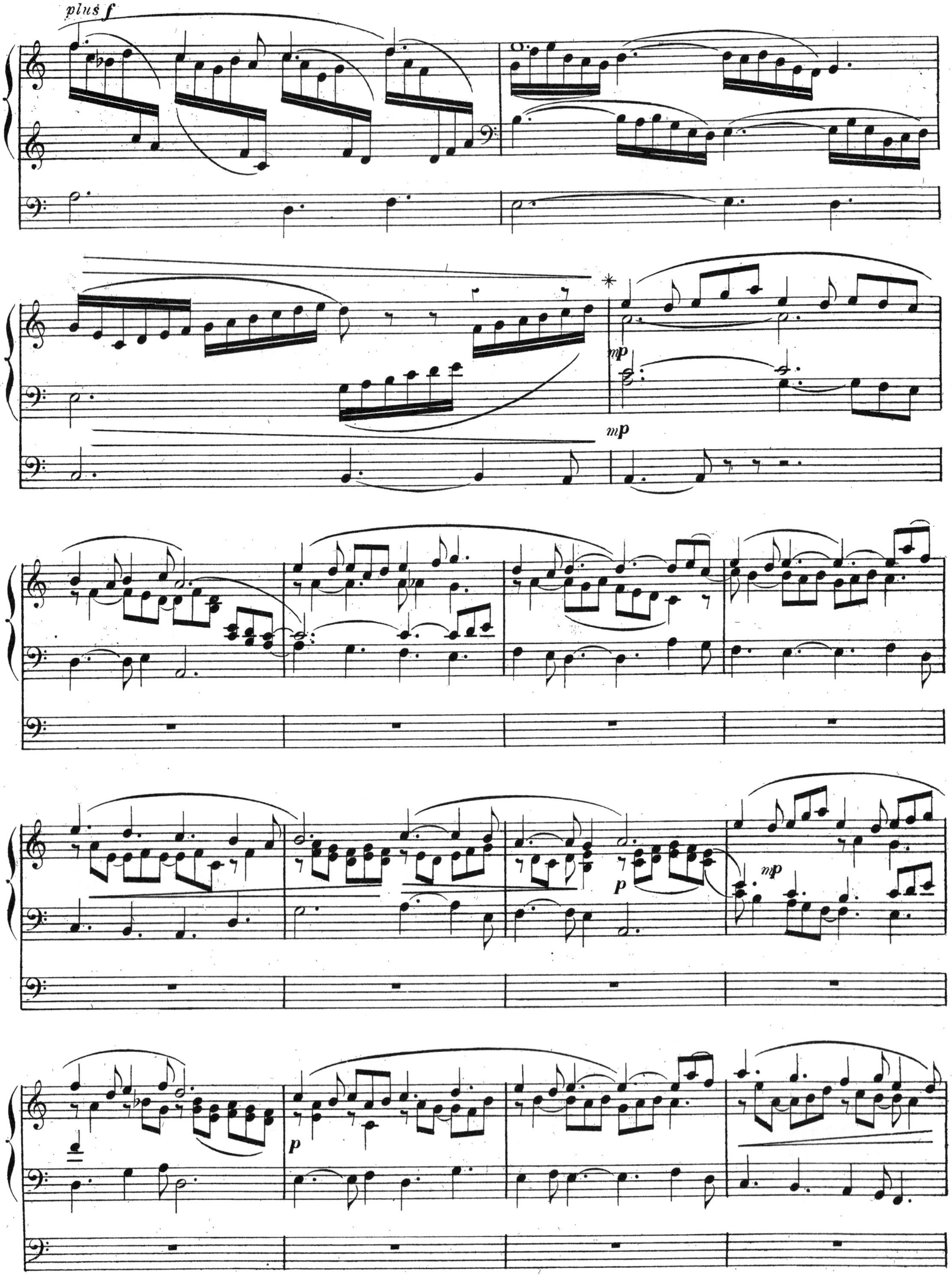

* A l'office on peut passer à la 2 *

45

en augmentant.

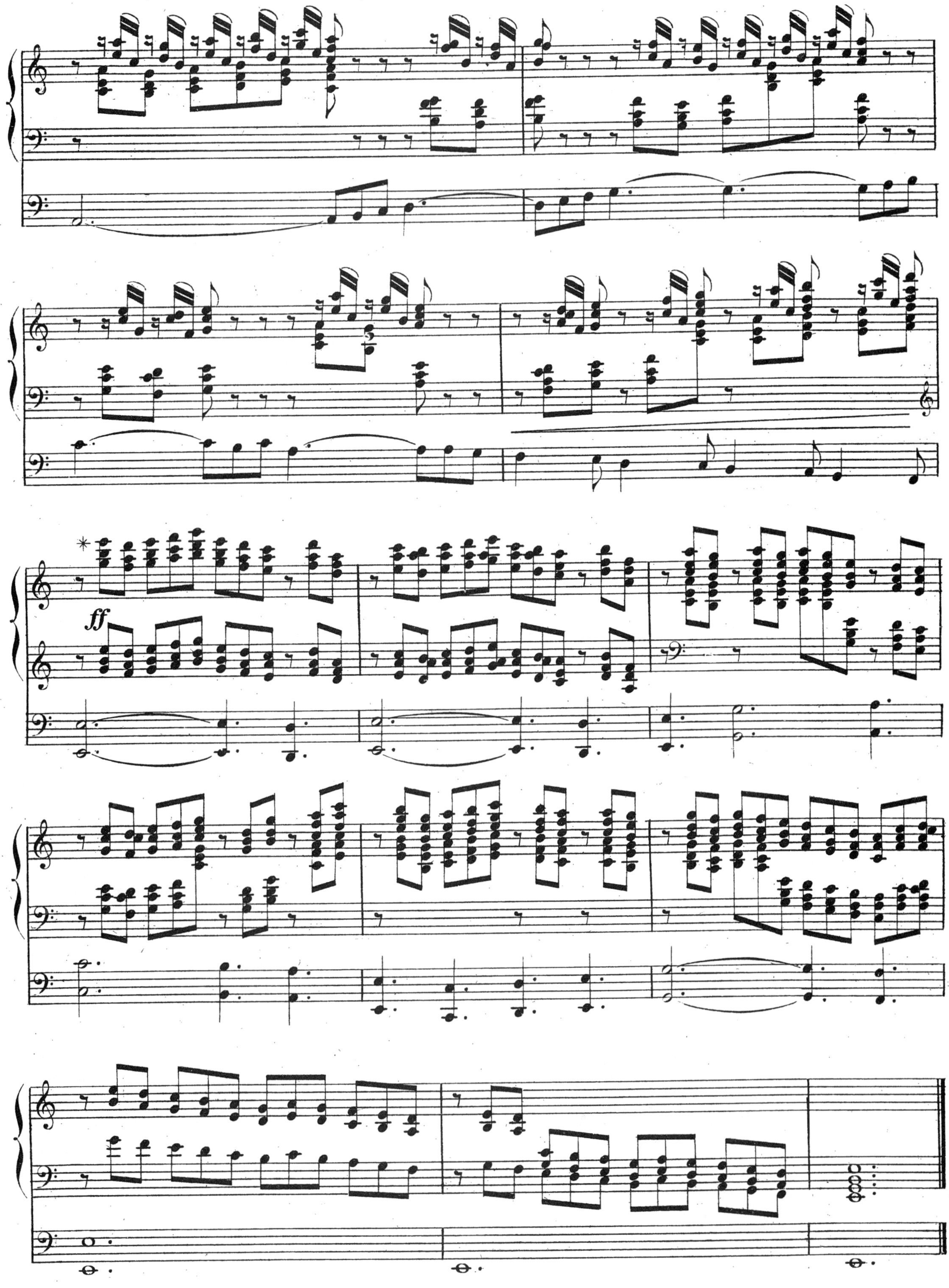
ff

VIII
Veni Sponsa Christi
Antienne du 7ᵉ Mode.

Modéré.

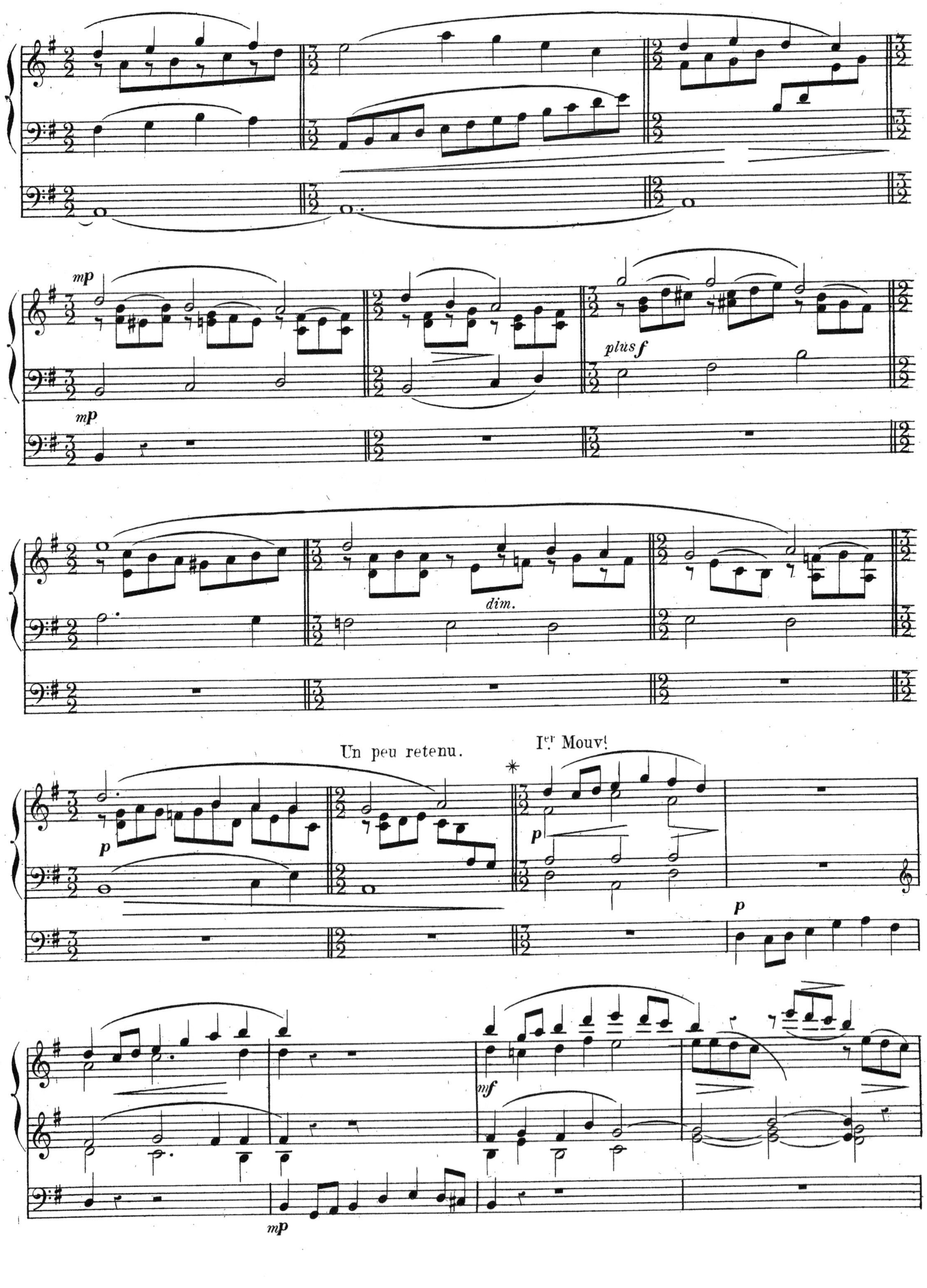
mp
mp
plus f
dim.
Un peu retenu.
Ier Mouvt
p
p
p
mp
mf

49

San Domenico di Fiesole
Janvier 1898

Autres antiennes brêves pour le Magnificat

I Modéré.

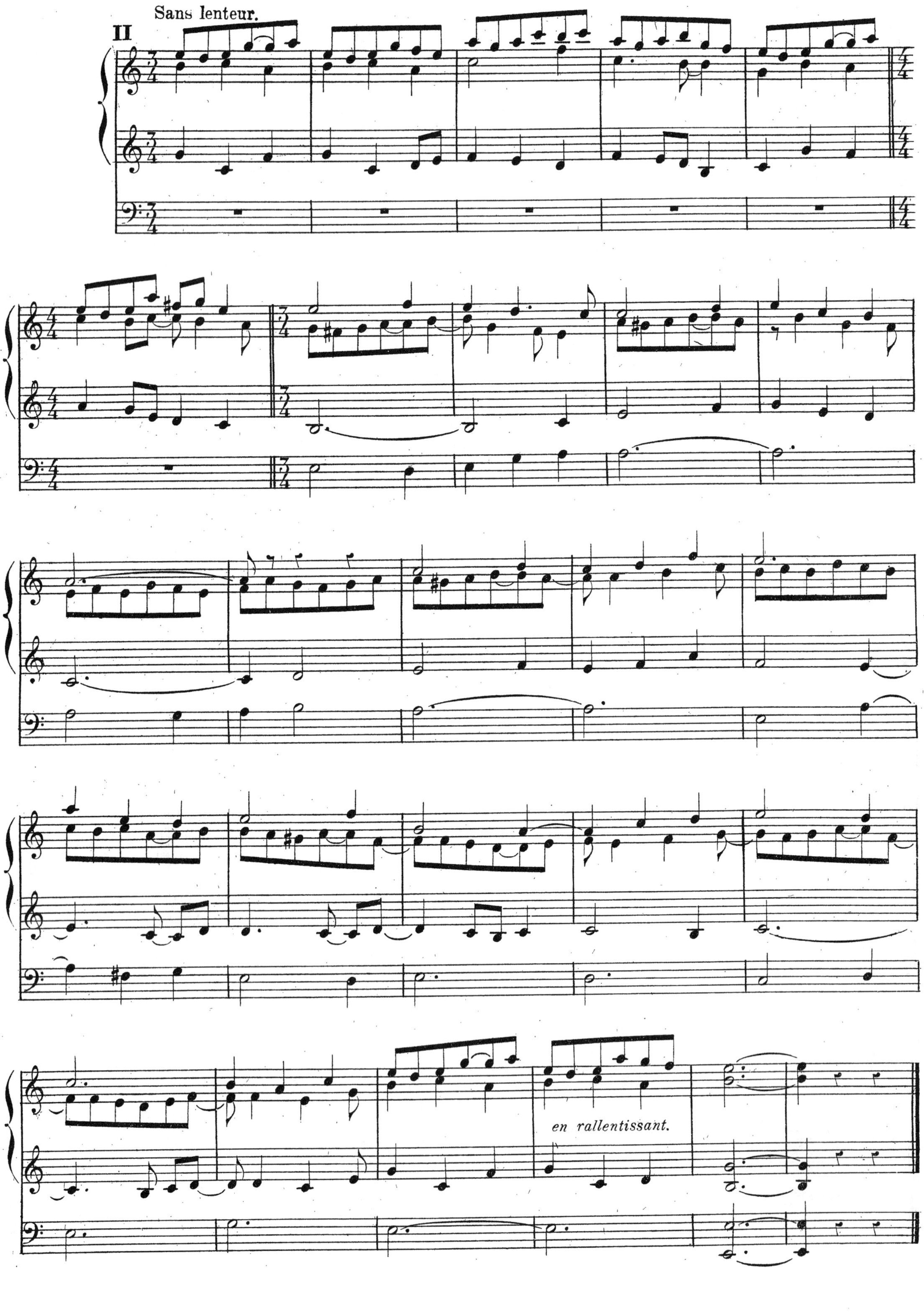
Sans lenteur.
II
en rallentissant.

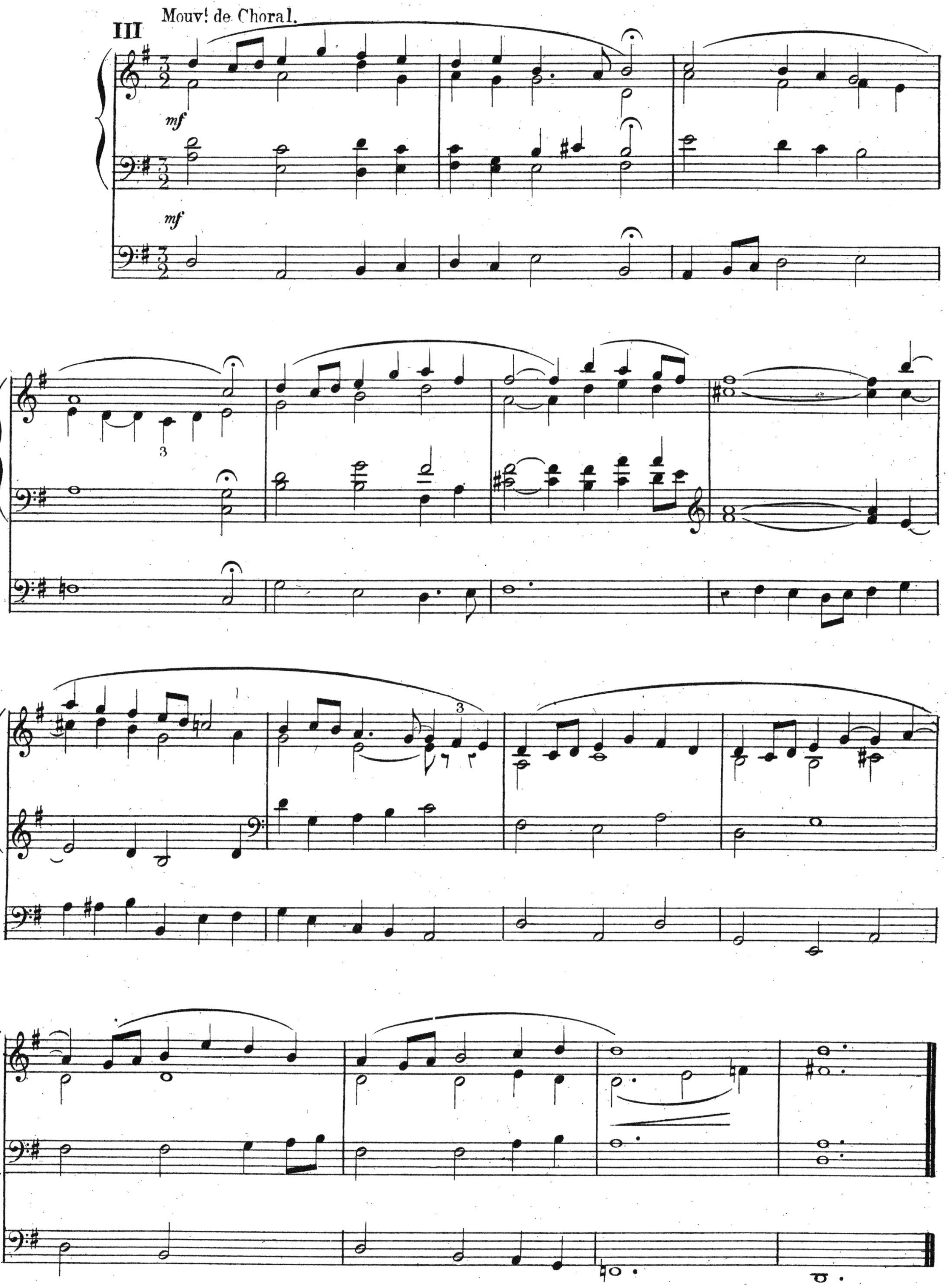
Mouv! de Choral.
III
3
2
mf
mf
3
3

SUITE GOTHIQUE

Op. 25

LÉON BOËLLMANN
1862–1897

I

INTRODUCTION – CHORAL

Fonds et Anches 4. 8. 16 à tous les claviers

Maestoso ♩ = 50

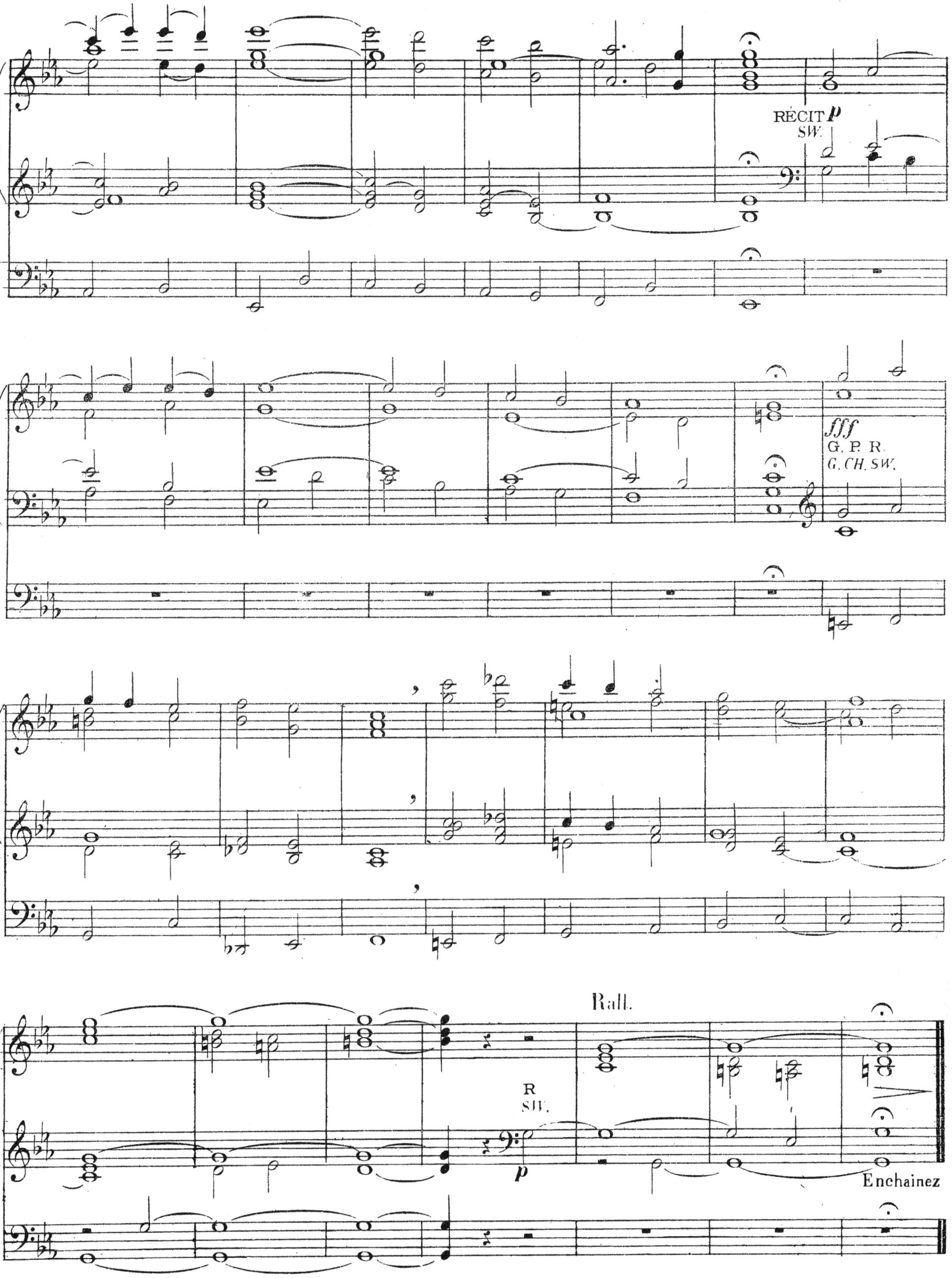
RÉCIT p
SW.
fff
G. P. R.
G. CH. SW.
Rall.
R
SW.
p
Enchainez

II

MENUET GOTHIQUE

Fonds et Anches 4. 8. 16 à tous les claviers

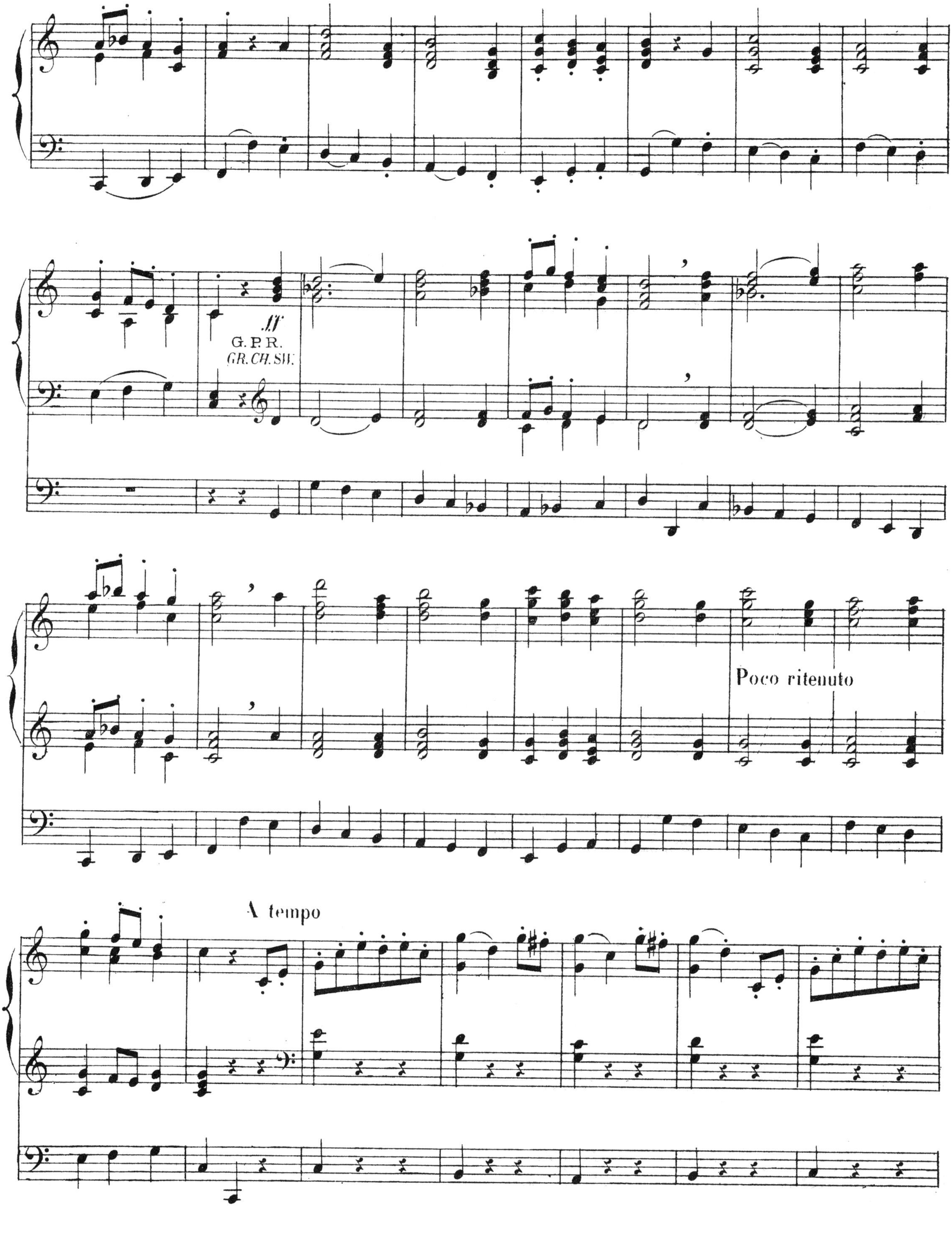
ff
G. P. R.
GR. CH. SW.
Poco ritenuto
A tempo

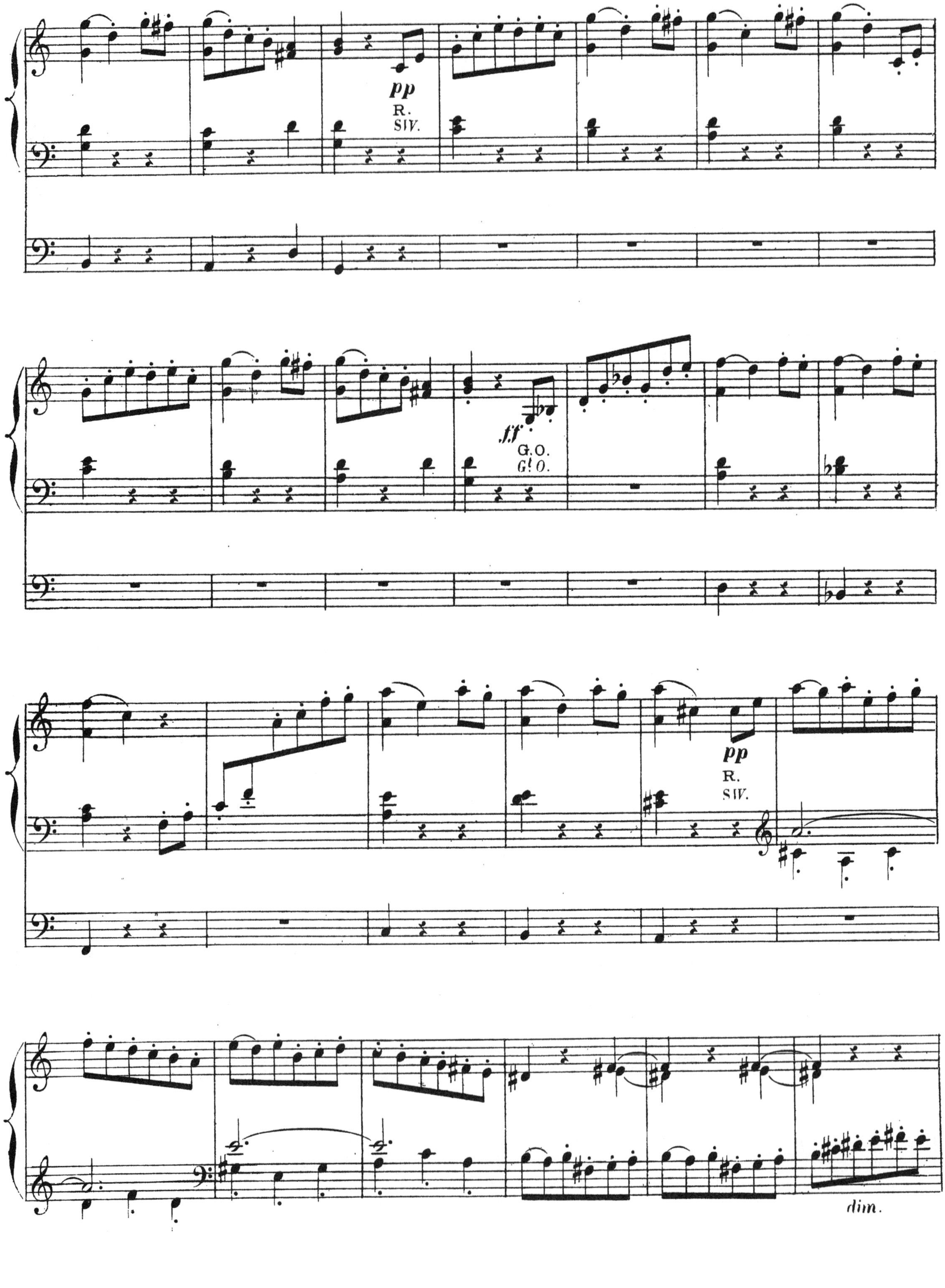
pp
R.
SW.
ff
G.O.
Gt O.
pp
R.
SW.
dim.

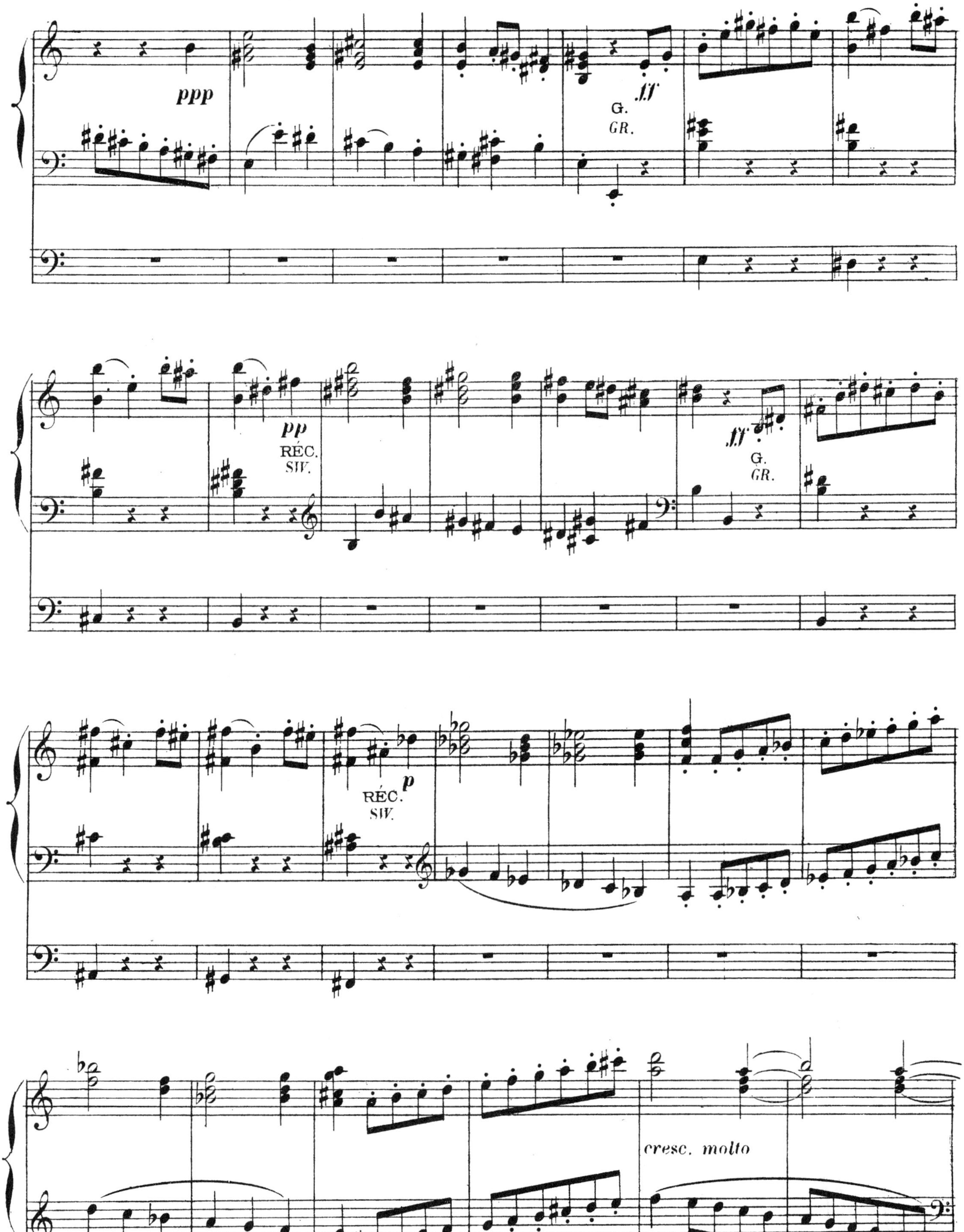
ppp
ff
G.
GR.
pp
RÉC.
SW.
ff
G.
GR.
RÉC.
SW.
p
cresc. molto

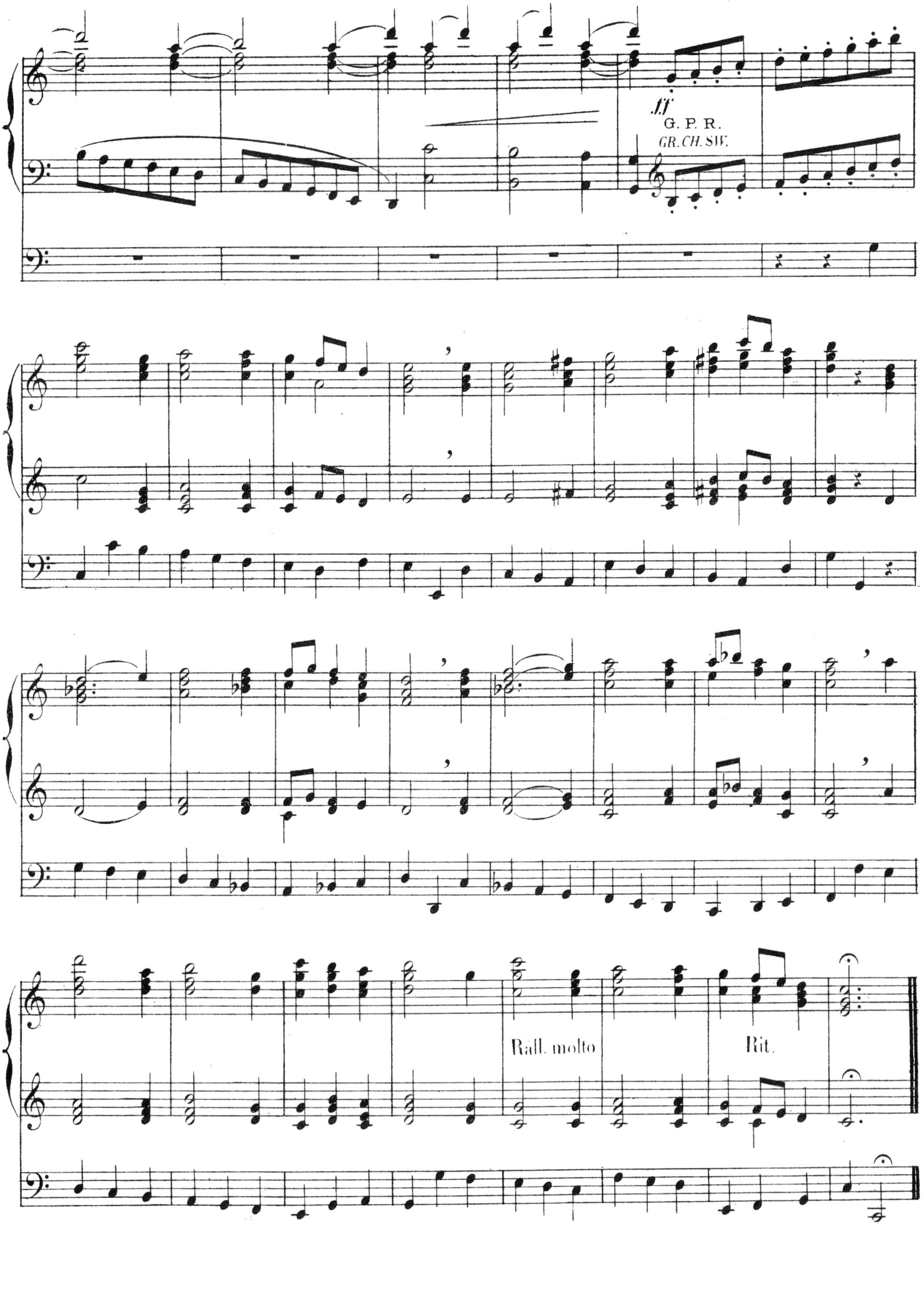
ff
G. P. R.
GR. CH. SW.
Rall. molto
Rit.

III
PRIÈRE À NOTRE-DAME

RÉCIT: Gambe et Voix céleste
G^d. – ORGUE: Flûte ou Bourdon 8
PÉDALE: Basses douces 8, 16

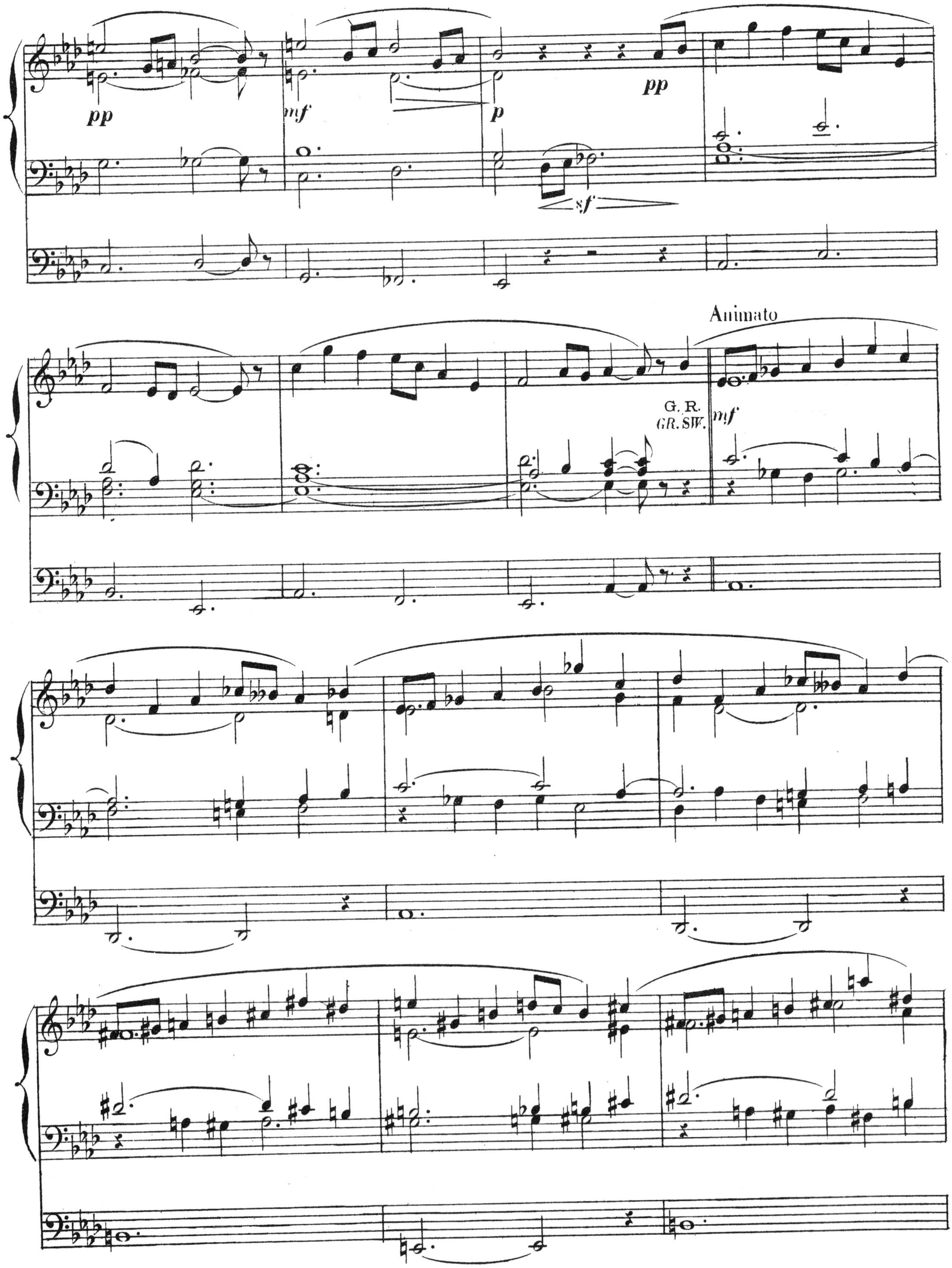
pp
mf
p
pp
sf
Animato
G. R.
GR. SW.
mf

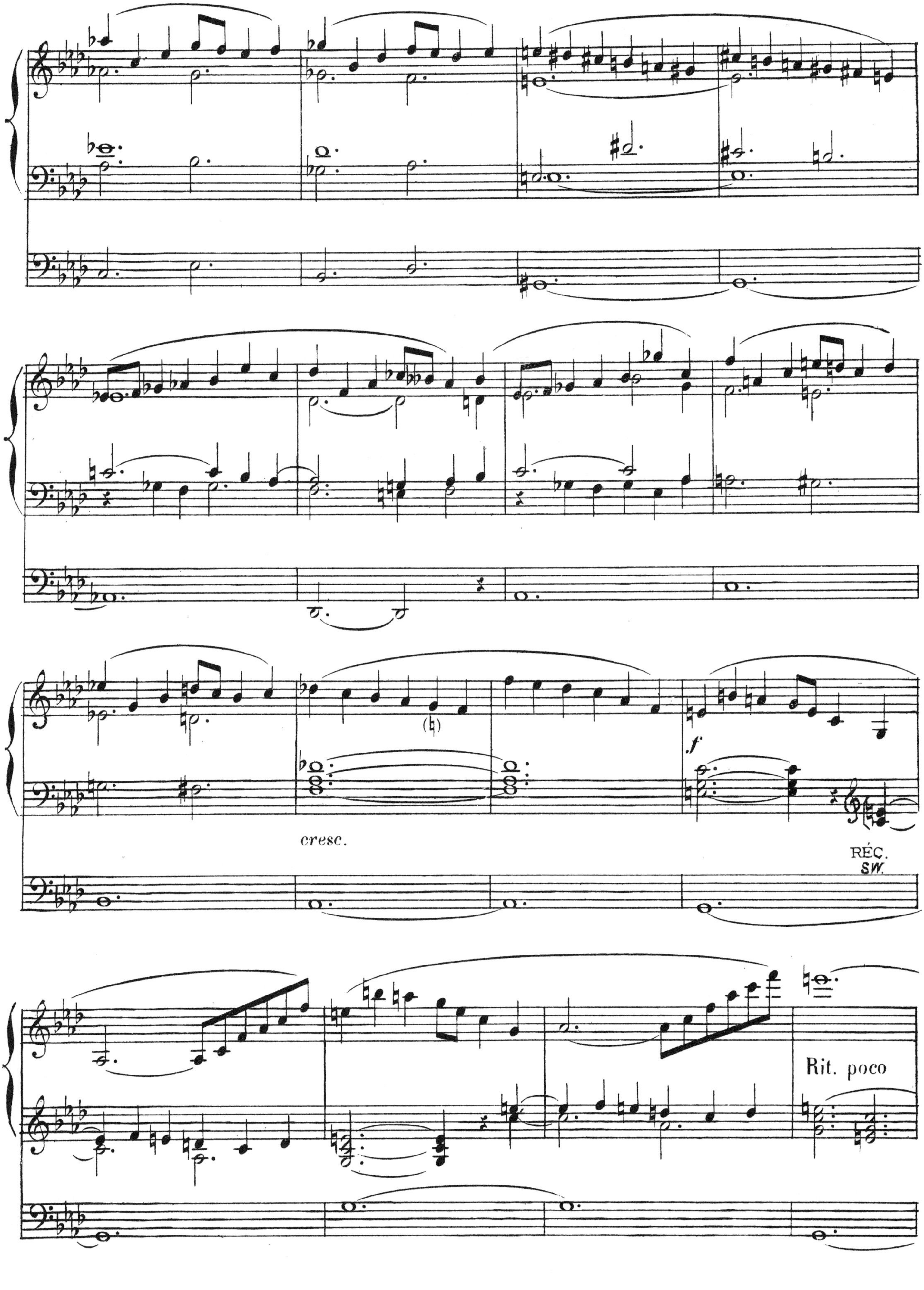
(♮)
f
cresc.
RÉC.
SW.
Rit. poco

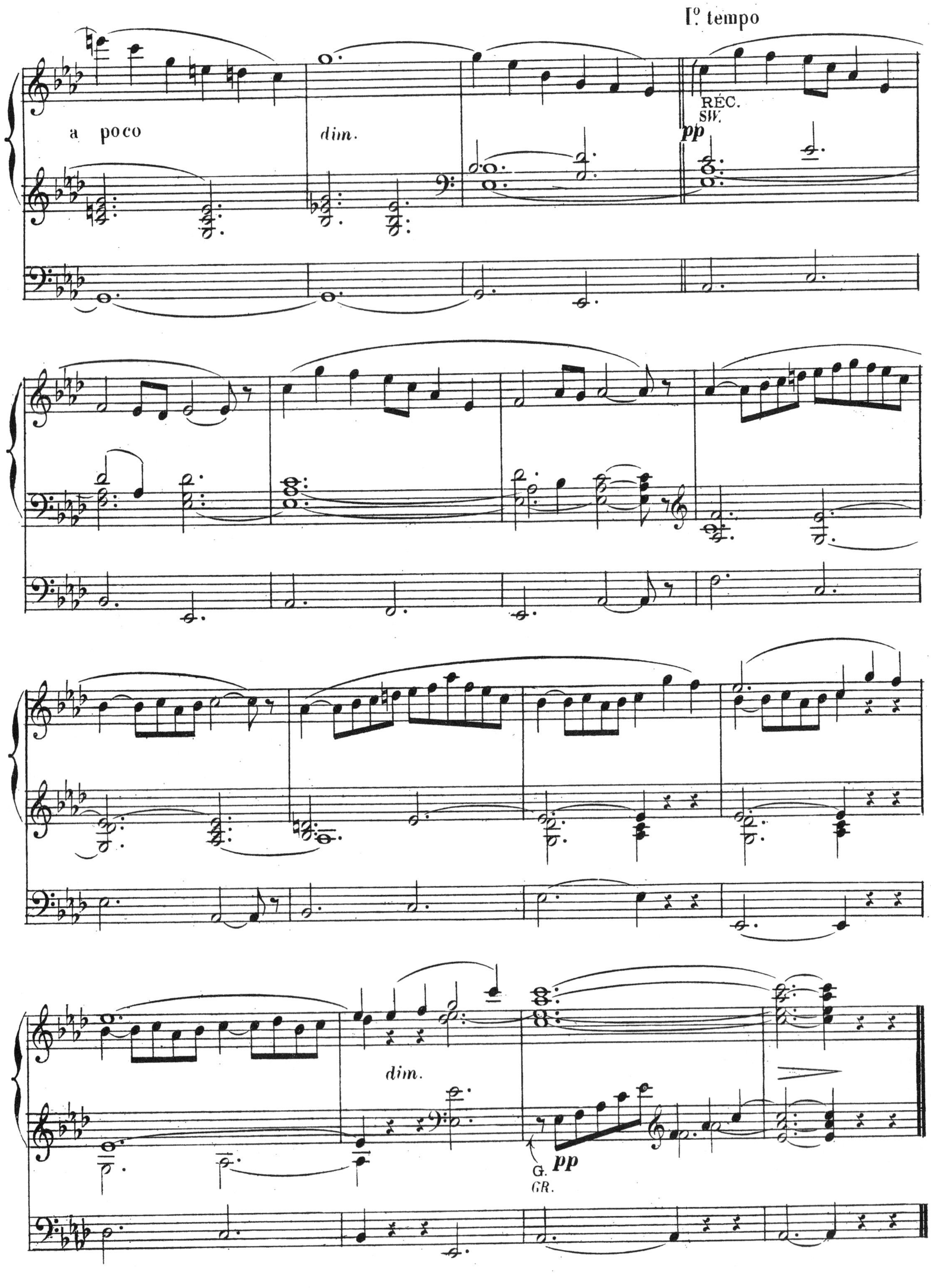
I°. tempo
a poco
dim.
RÉC.
SW.
pp
dim.
G.
GR.
pp

IV
Toccata

RÉCIT: Fonds et Anches 4, 8.

POSITIF: Fonds 4, 8 (Anches 4, 8 préparées)

G^{d}. – ORGUE: Fonds 4, 8 (Anches 4, 8, 16 préparées)

PÉDALE: Fonds 4, 8, 16, 32, Tirasses (Anches préparées)

Allegro ♩ = 132

MANUALE

RÉC.
SIV. *pp leggierissimo*

PÉDALE

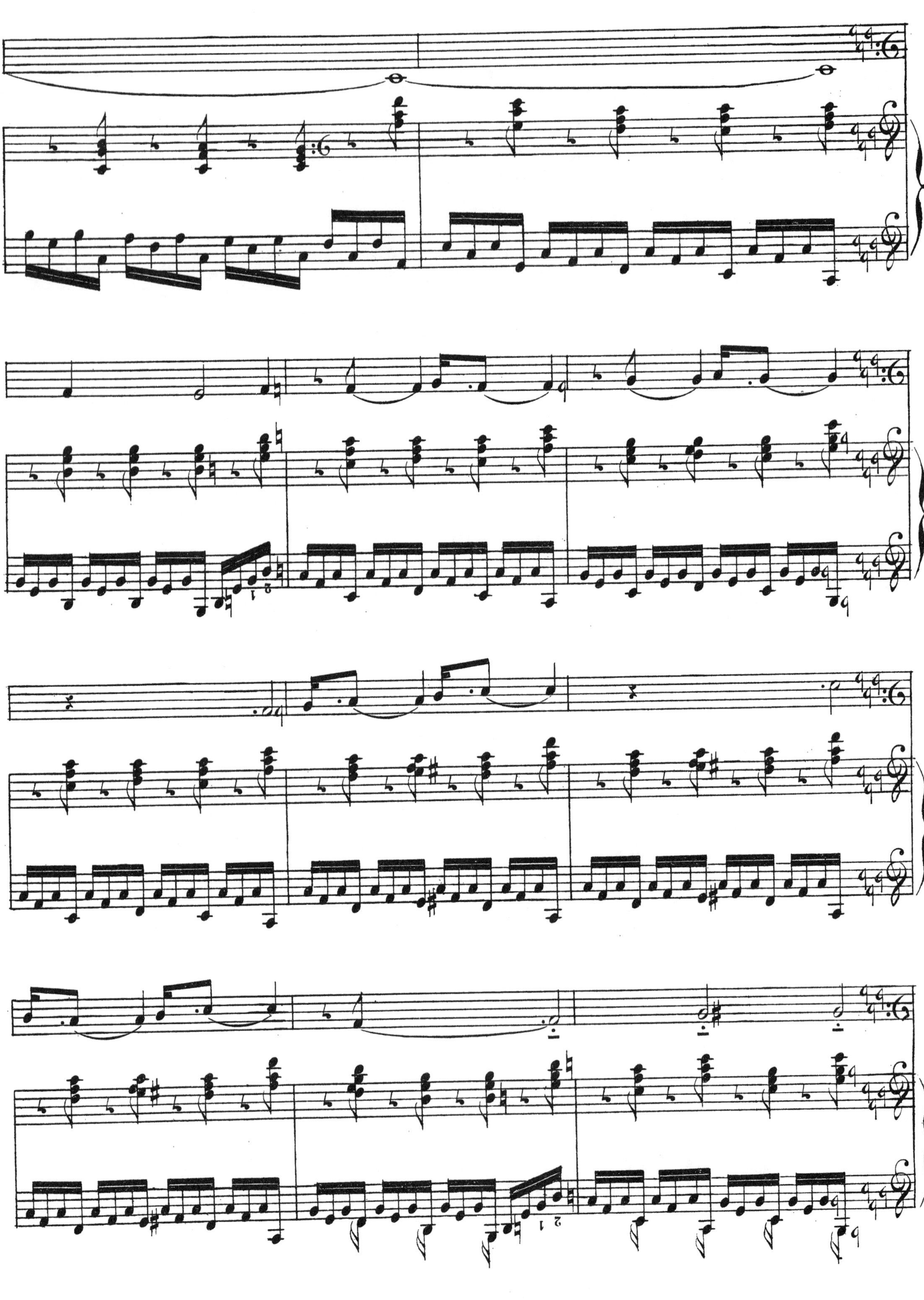

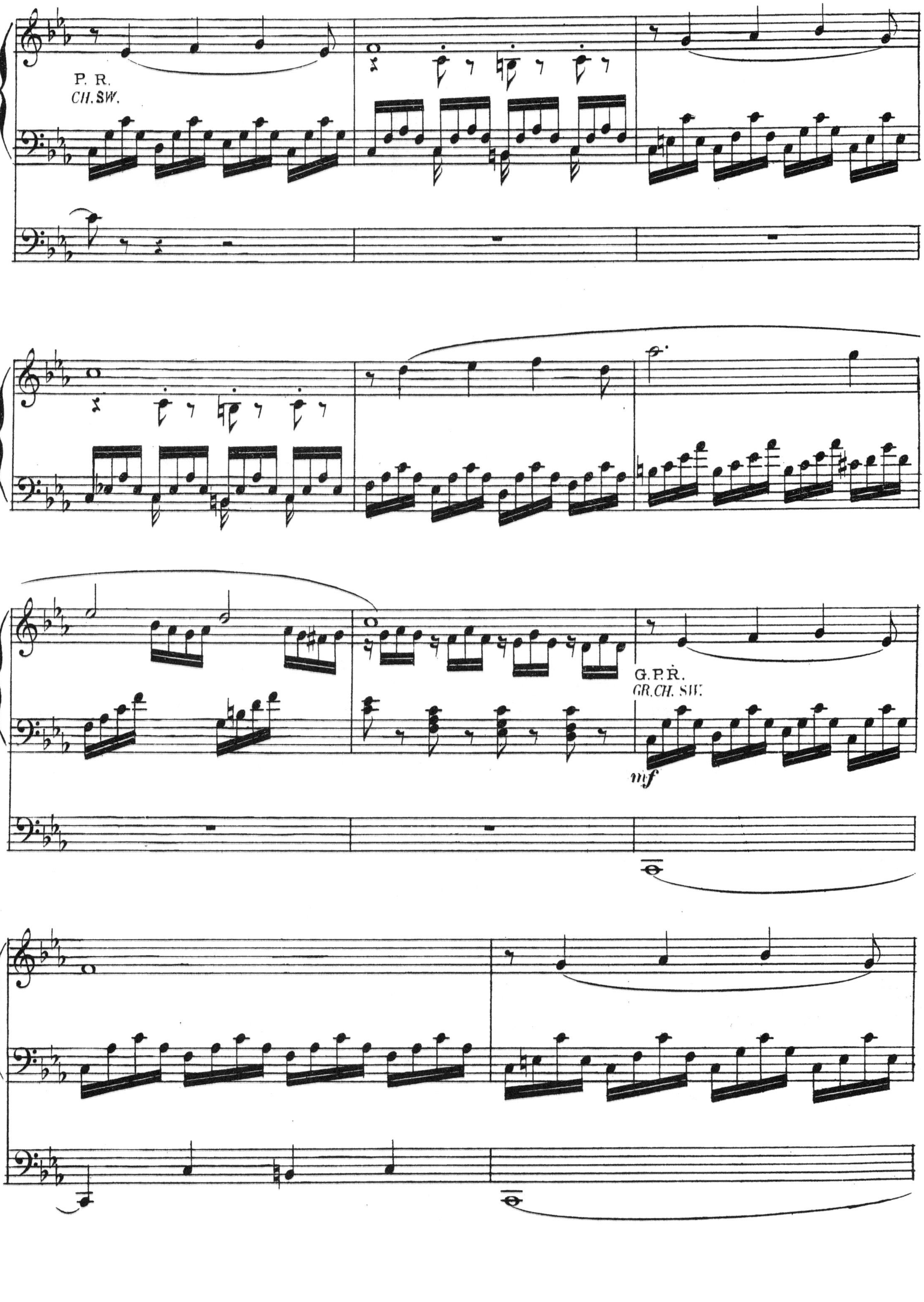
P. R.
CH. SW.
G.P.R.
GR. CH. SW.
mf

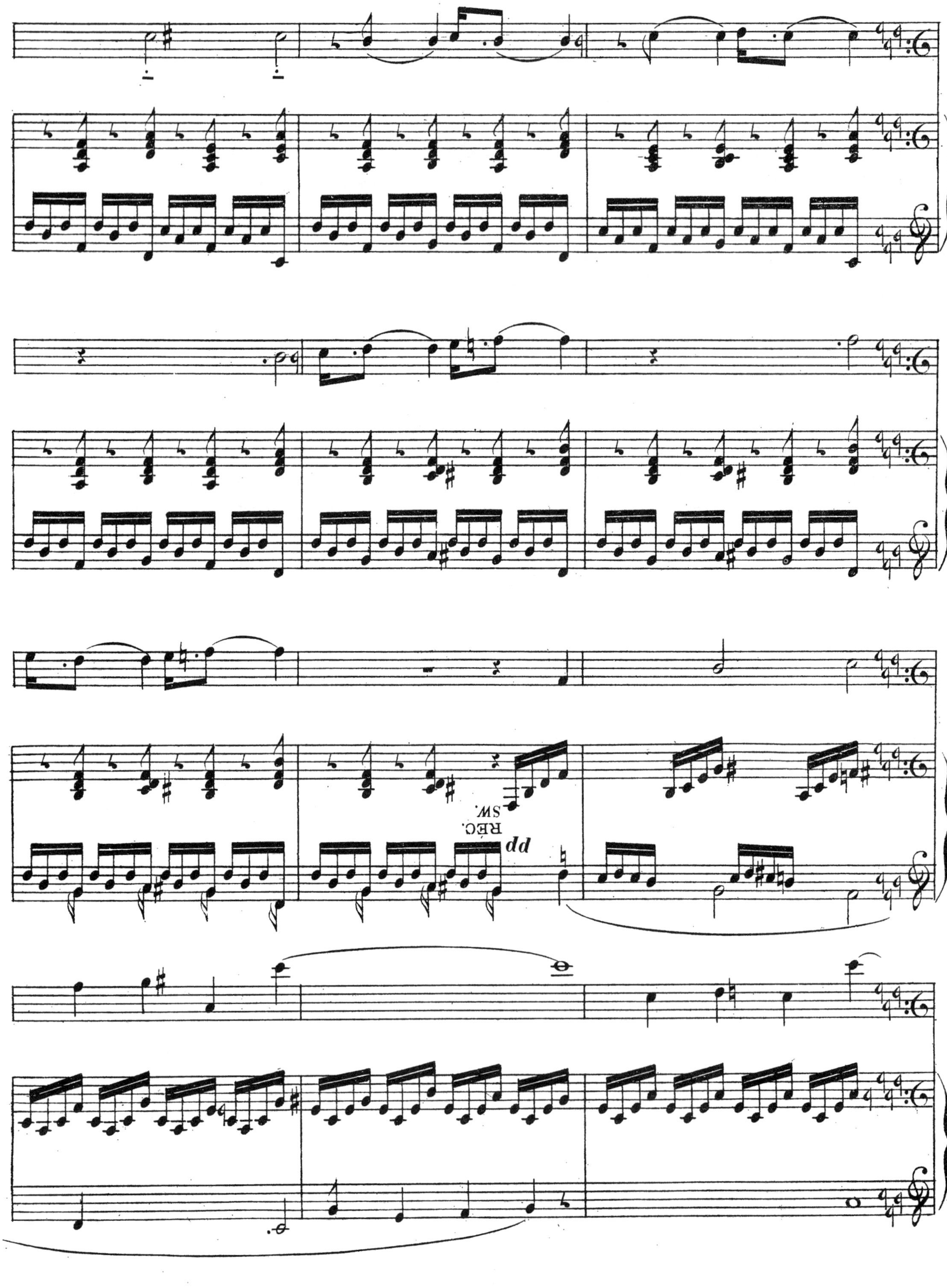
pp
RÉC.
SW.

69

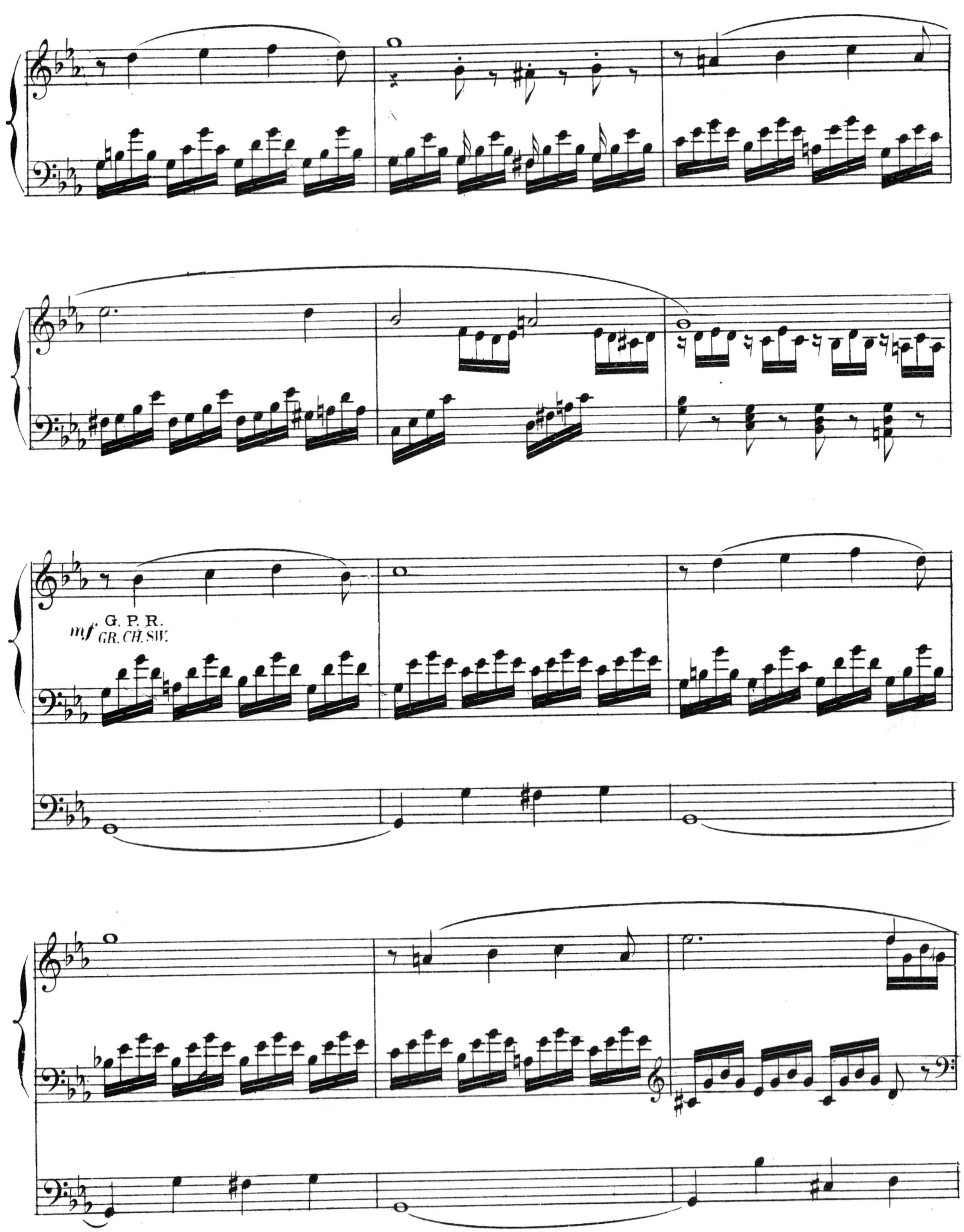
mf G. P. R.
GR. CH. SW.

cresc.
Anches Pos.
CH. Reeds add
cresc.
cresc.
Anches G.
GR. Reeds add
cresc.
ff
Anches Ped.
PED. Reeds

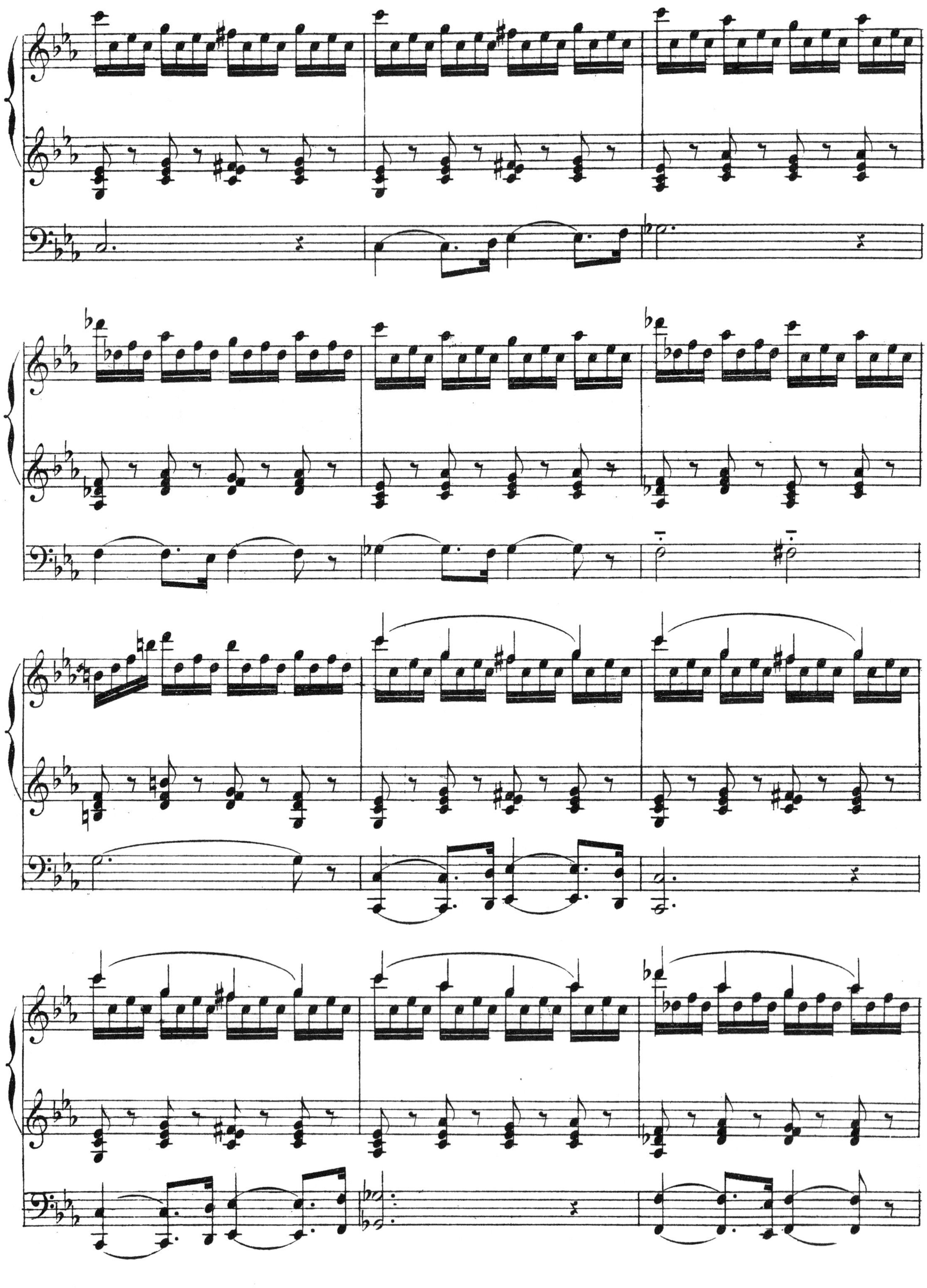

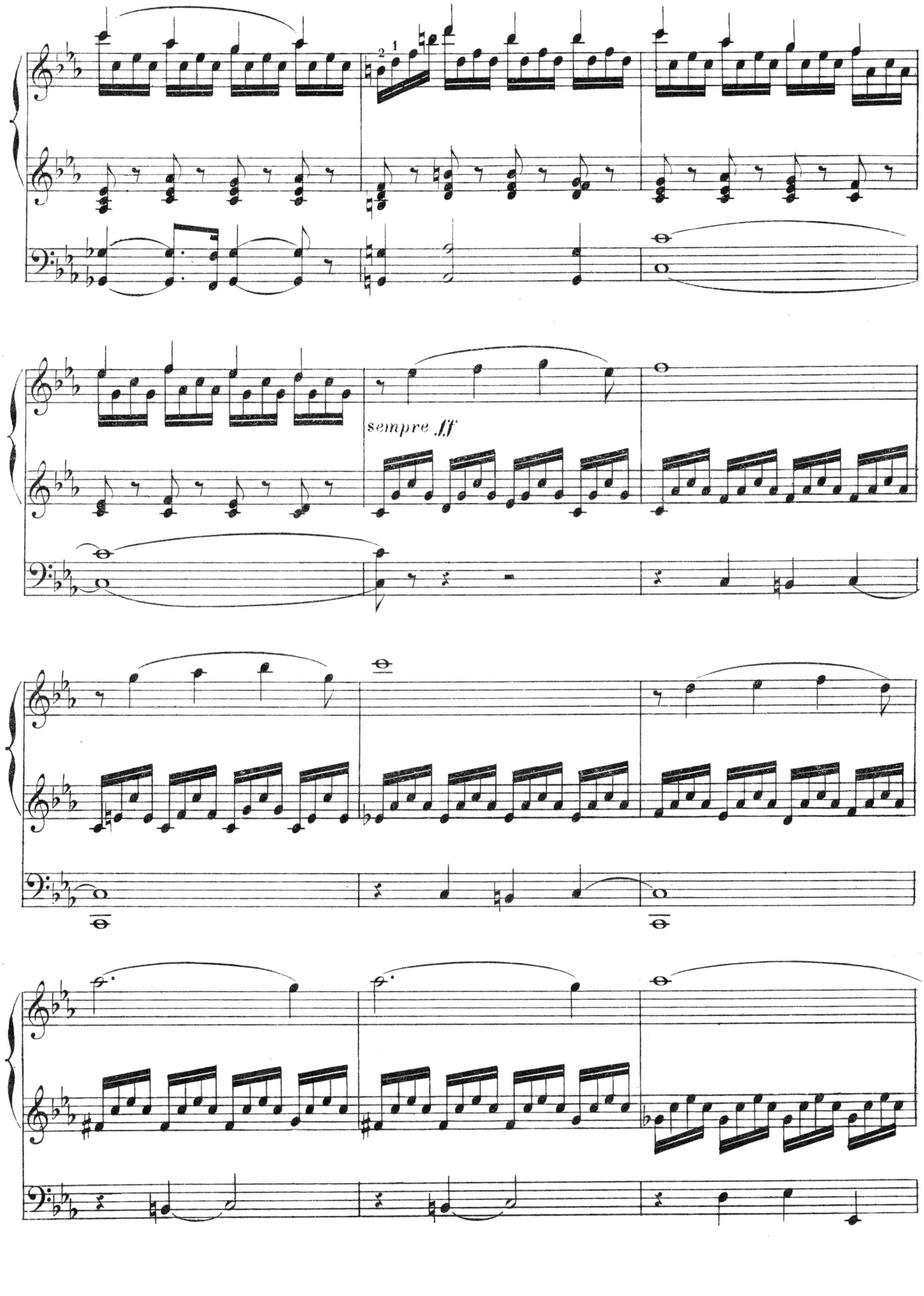
2
1
sempre ff

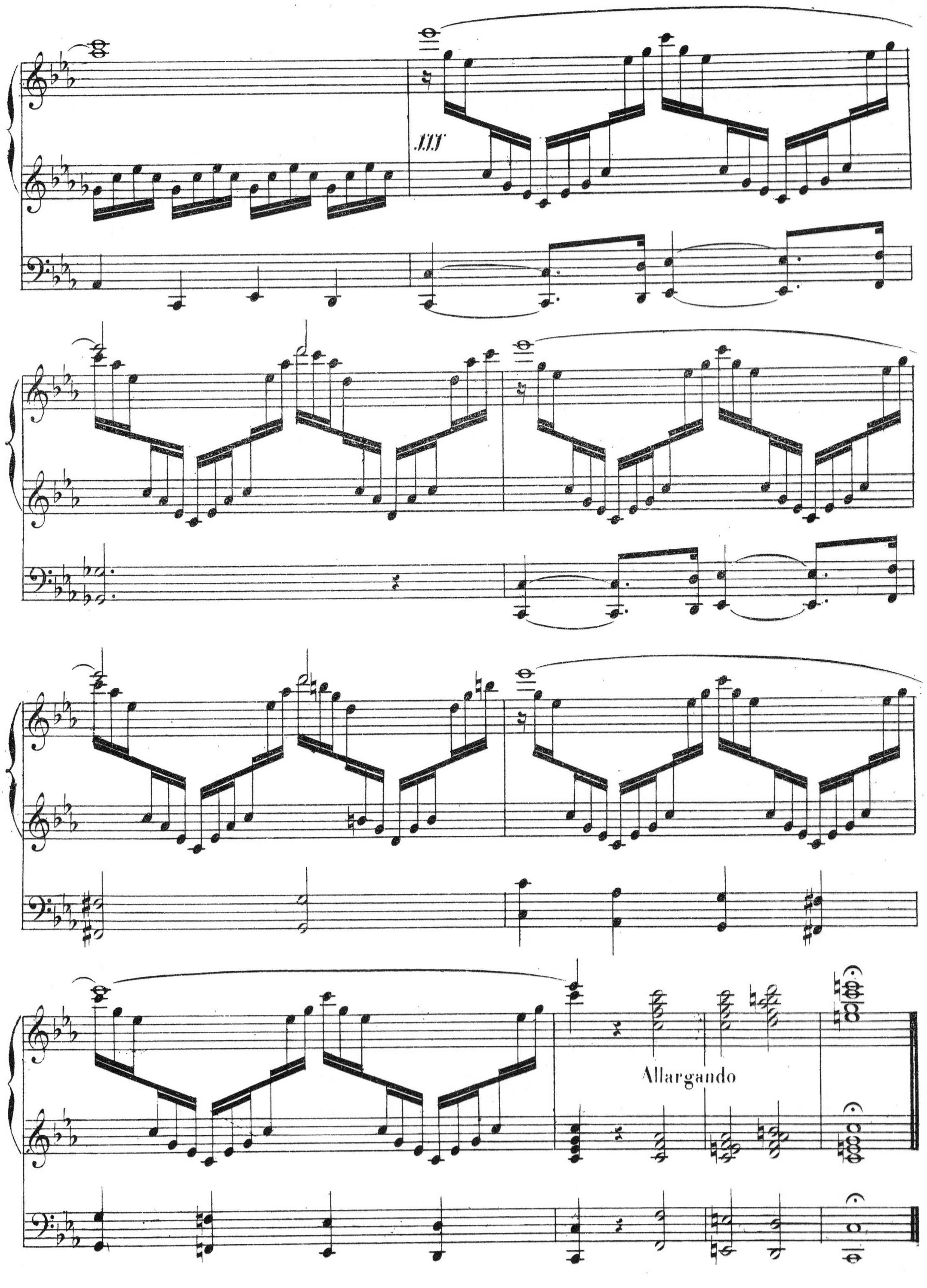

Allargando

TROIS PIÈCES

Op. 29

A Monsieur SAMUEL ROUSSEAU

Maître de Chapelle de S^{te}. Clotilde

GABRIEL PIERNÉ
1863–1937

I

PRÉLUDE

RÉCIT   Gambe 8, Bourdon 8, Fl. Anches préparées
POSITIF   Bourdon 8, Flûte 8, Montre 8. Anches préparées sans 16 P.
G.-O.   Flûte 8. Bourdon 8. Anches préparées
PÉD.   Octave 8 et 16. Anches préparées

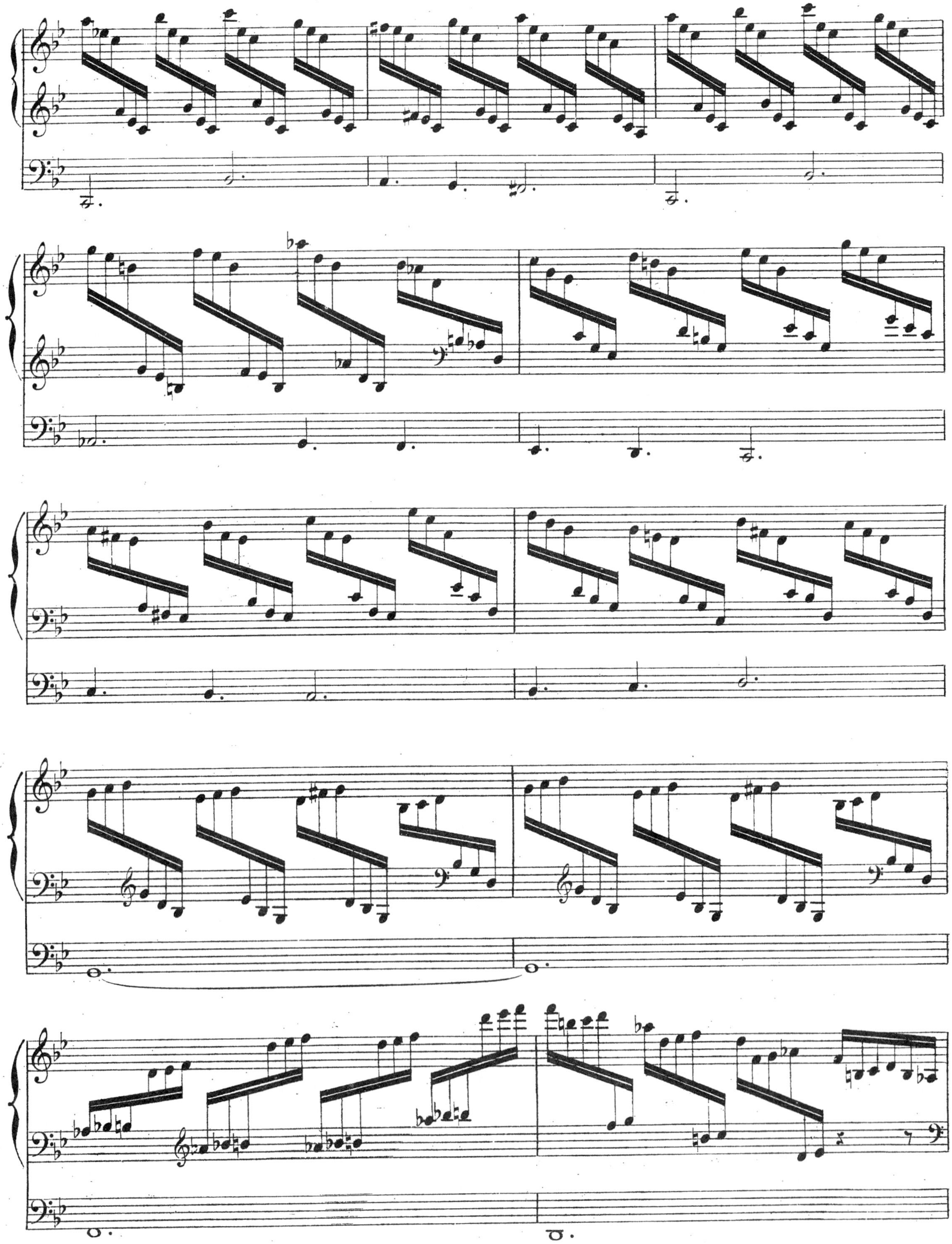

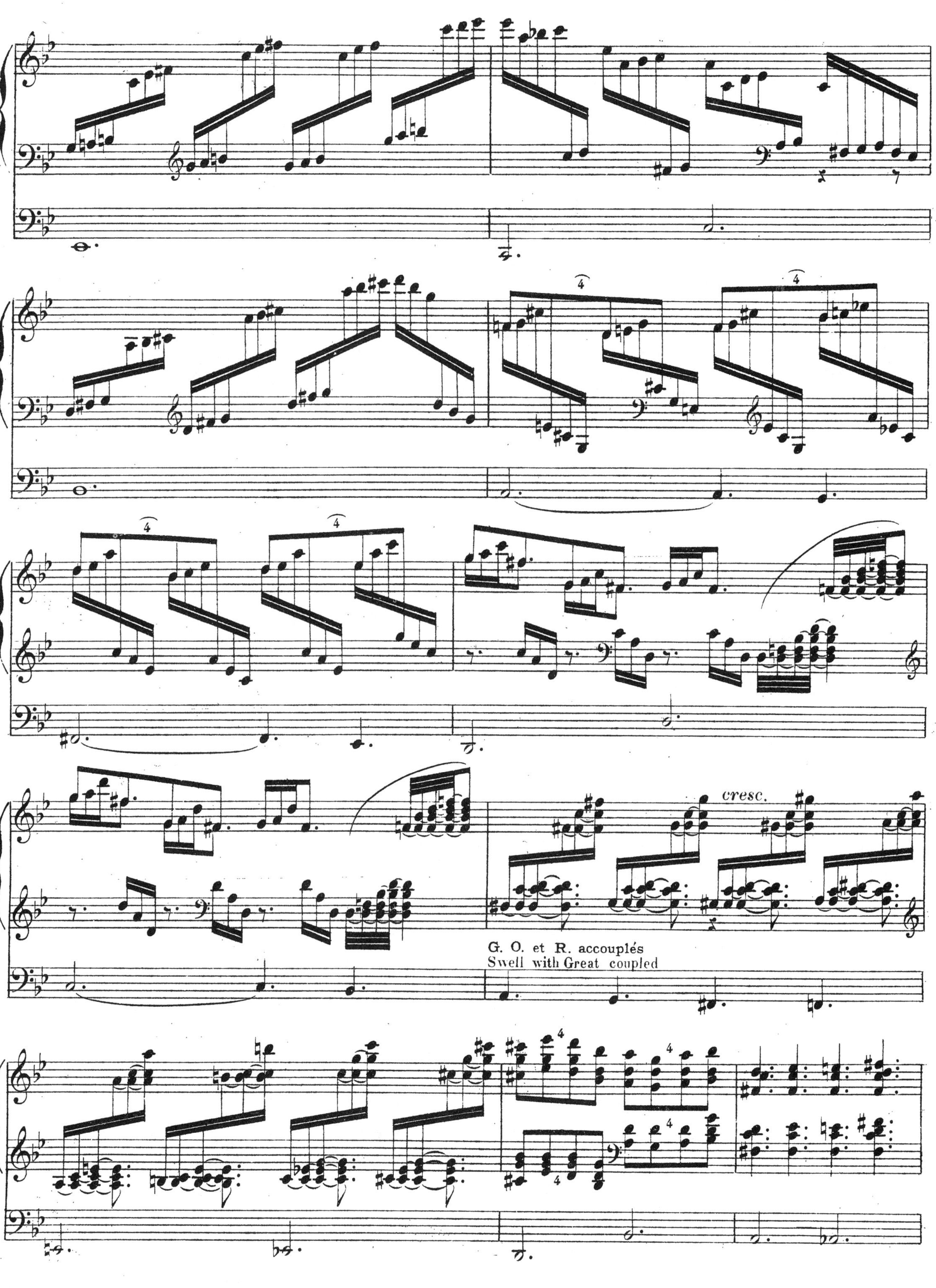
cresc.
G. O. et R. accouplés
Swell with Great coupled

Anches Récit
Swell Reeds

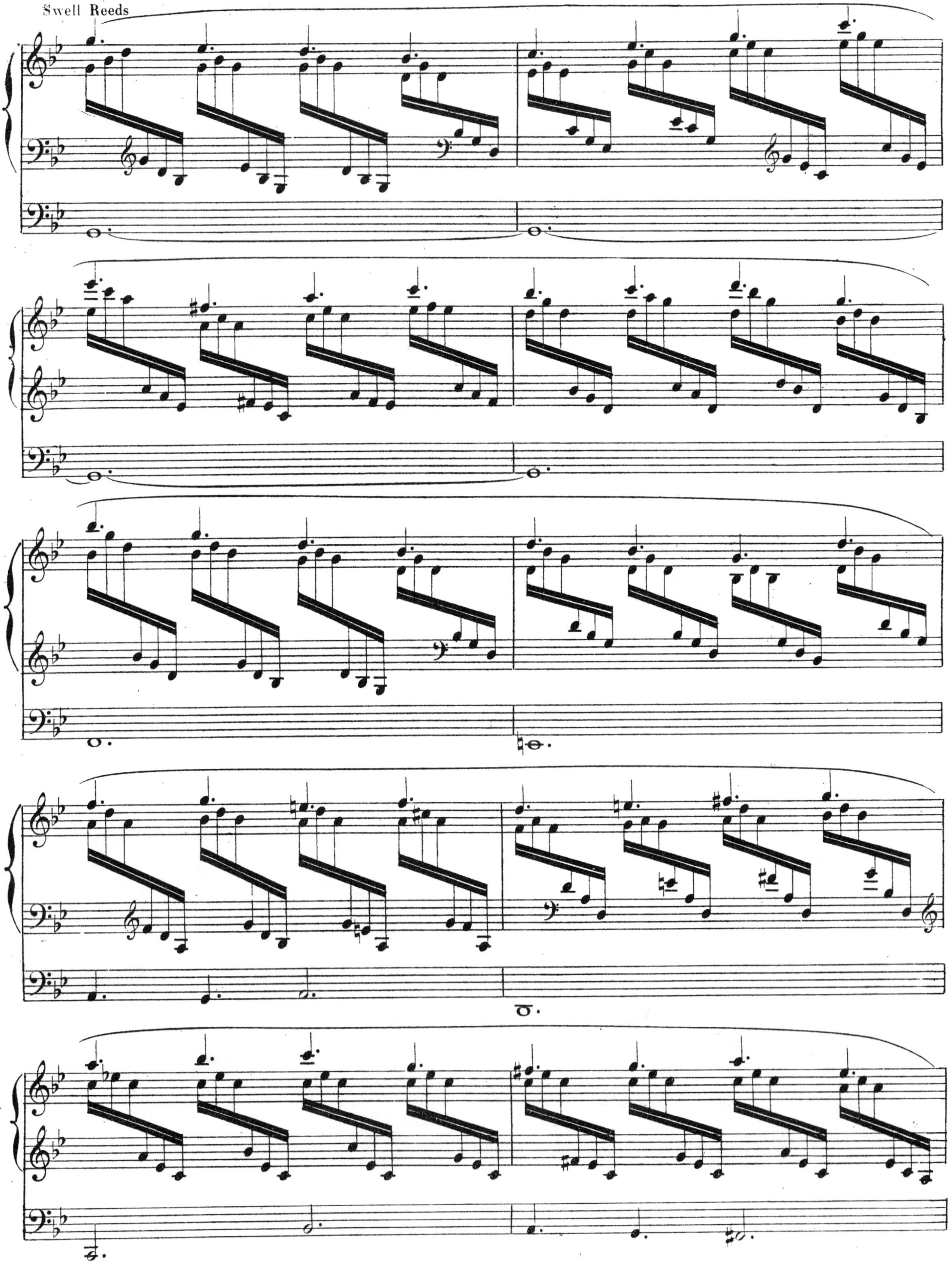

Anches Pos.
Choir Redds
Anches G. O.
Great Redds
Anches Pos.
Pedal Redds

À Monsieur Thèodore DUBOIS
Organiste du G^d Orgue de la Madeleine

II

CANTILÈNE

RÉCIT   Flûte 8, Bourdon 8, Trompette (trémolo)
POSITIF   Bourdon 8
G.-O.   Bourdon 8
PÉD.   Fonds 8 et 16

p
ajoutez la Flûte de 8 au Pos. accouplez Récit au Pos.
Choir add. Flûte 8 Choir and Swell coupled

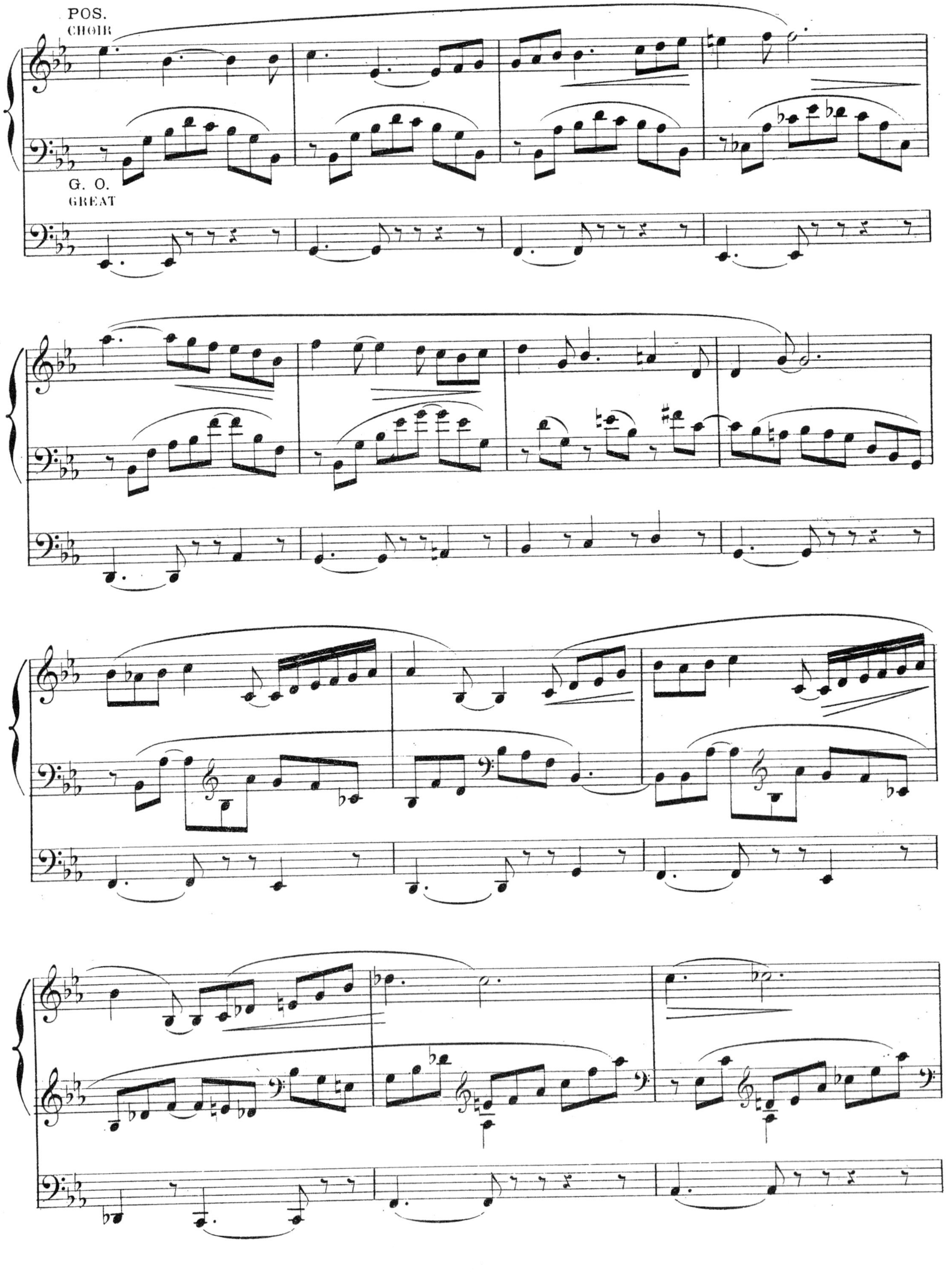
POS.
CHOIR
G. O.
GREAT

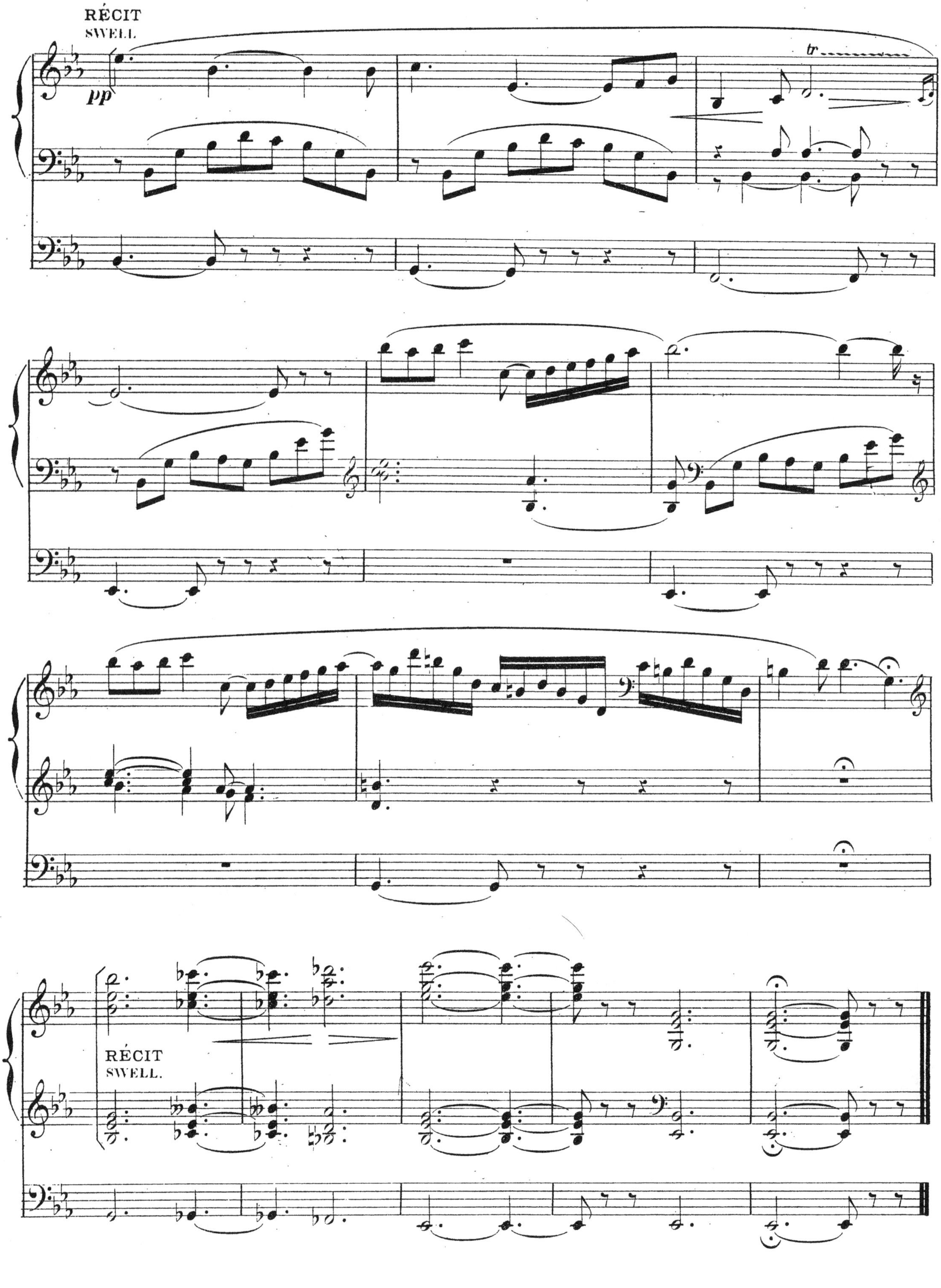

RÉCIT
SWELL
pp
tr
RÉCIT
SWELL.

À Monsieur ALEXANDRE GUILMANT
Organiste du G^d Orgue de la Trinité

III

SCHERZANDO

de Concert

RÉCIT   Hautbois, Flûte 8, Trompette
POSITIF   Bourdon 8, Anches préparées
G.-O.   Flûte 8, Bourdon 8, Montre 8. Anches préparées
PÉD.   Fonds 8, 16, et 4. Anches préparées
       Positif et G.-O. accouplés

ôtez trompette
cornopean in

(boîte ouverte,

(open box)

POS.
CHOIR

RÉCIT

RÉCIT
SWELL

RÉCIT
SWELL

POS.

CHOIR

POS.
CHOIR

RÉCIT
SWELL

RÉCIT
SWELL

POS.

CHOIR

Tirasse du G. O.
Great to Pedal

G. O.
GREAT

RÉCIT
SWELL

RÉCIT
SWELL

ôtez la tirasse
Pedal uncoupled

mettez Fl. oct. au Récit (boite ouverte)
Swel add Flute 4 (open box)

87

POS.
CHOIR

RÉCIT
SWELL

POS.
CHOIR

POS.
CHOIR

RÉCIT
SWELL

RÉCIT
SWELL

POS.
CHOIR

RÉCIT
SWELL

tirasse G. O.
Great to Pedal

G. O.
GREAT

RÉCIT
SWELL

G. O.
GREAT

RÉCIT
SWELL

POS.
CHOIR

ôtez tirasse
Pedal uncoupled

RÉCIT   otez H^b mettez
Tromp. et Tremolo

Un poco meno

SWELL   Oboe in   add. Cornopean
tremulant

RÉCIT (boite fermée)
SWELL   (shut box)

POS.
CHOIR

(boite ouverte)
(open box)

RÉCIT
SWELL

POS.
CHOIR

RÉCIT
SWELL

POS.
CHOIR

RÉCIT
SWELL

ôtez trémolo
tremulant in

POS.
CHOIR

RÉCIT
SWELL

POS.
CHOIR

RÉCIT
SWELL

RÉCIT   mettez H.^b et Fl. oct. ôtez Tromp.
SWELL   Cornopean in add. Oboe & Flute 4

POS.
CHOIR
RÉCIT
SWELL
POS.
CHOIR
POS.
CHOIR
RÉCIT
SWELL
RÉCIT
SWELL
POS.
CHOIR
Tirasse G. O.
Great to Pedal

RECIT. mettez Anches (boite fermée)
POS. ajoutez tous les fonds de 8
SWELL. add Reeds (Shut box)
POS. all fundation stops 8
G. O.
GREAT
Accouplez Récit au G. O.
Great with Swell coupled
ôtez tirasse G.O.
Pedal uncoupled

RÉCIT (boite fermée)
SWELL (Shut box)
tirasse G. O.
Pedal to Great
G. O.
GREAT
Anches du Pos.
Choir Reeds
Anches Ped.
Pedal Reeds
Anches G. O.
Great Reedds

MESSE DES PAUVRES

ERIK SATIE
1866–1925

DESSUS
Ky - ri - e e - lé - - i - son Ky - -
BASSES
Ky - ri - e e - le - i - son
ORGUE DU CHŒUR
- ri - e e - lé - - i - son
GRAND ORGUE

96

BASSES
Christé e - lé - i - son
GRAND ORGUE
ORGUE DU CHŒUR
BASSES
Ky - ri - e e - lé - i - son

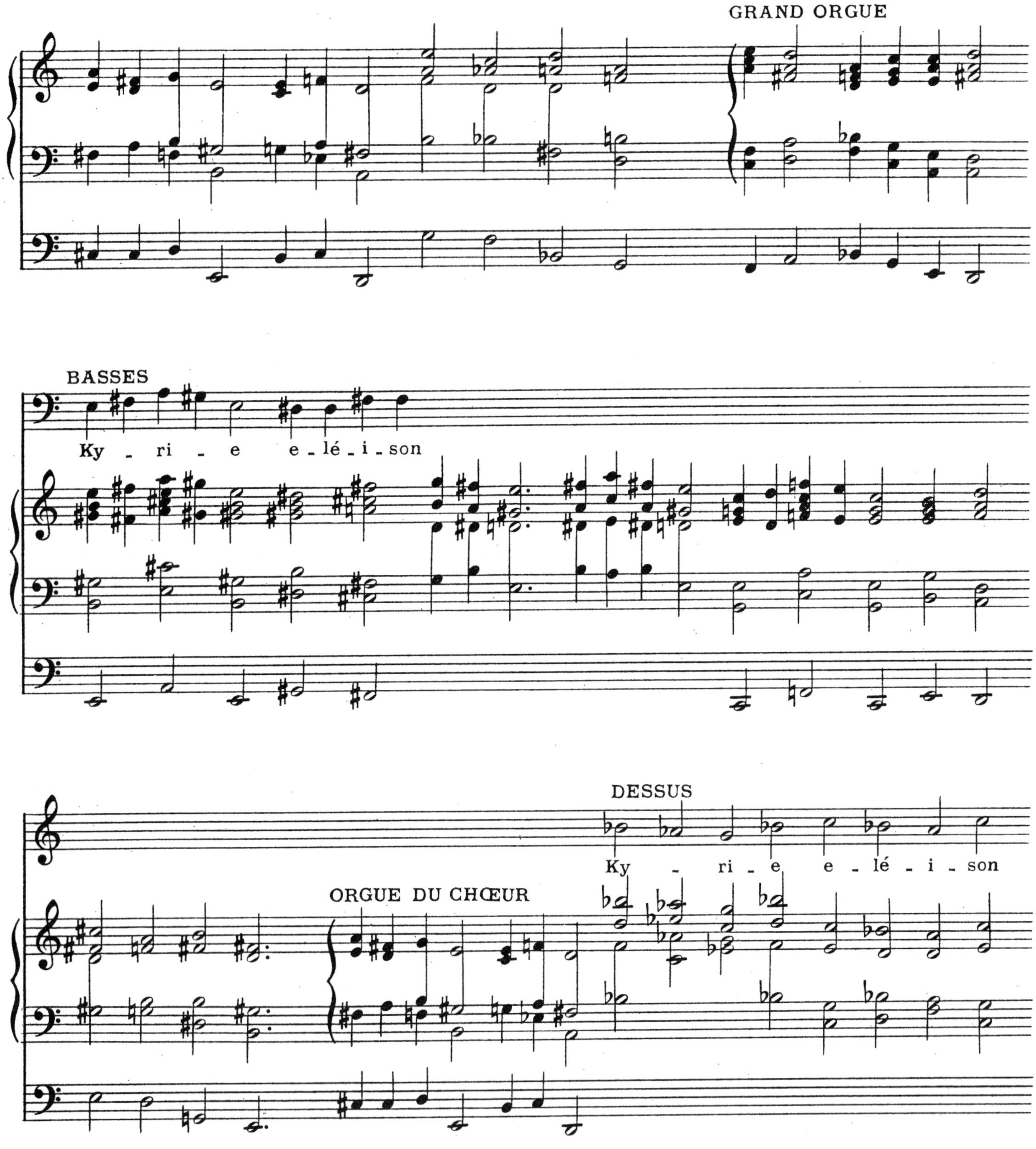

Dixit domine

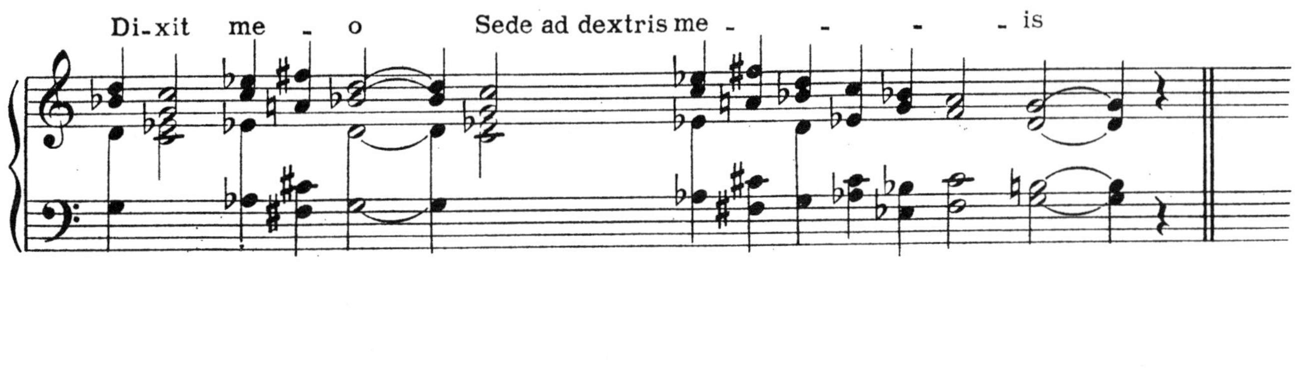

Prière des Orgues

PRAYER FOR ORGANS. *Very Christianly. Without ostentation. In the best. With a great forgetfulness of the present.*

In the best. With a great forgetfulness of the present. Very Christianly. Without ostentation. Unyielding.

Commune qui mundi nefas

On the inside. Truly. Without pride. Very well. Affirmative. The same affirmation but more internal. To apply oneself to renunciation. Very well. Almost invisible.

Chant Ecclésiastique

Prière pour les voyageurs et les marins en danger de mort,
à la très bonne et très auguste Vierge Marie, mère de Jésus.

ECCLESIASTICAL HYMN. PRAYER FOR TRAVELLERS AND SAILORS IN DANGER OF DEATH, TO THE VERY GOOD AND VERY AUGUST VIRGIN MARY, MOTHER OF JESUS.

PRAYER FOR THE SALVATION OF MY SOUL.

Prière pour le salut de mon âme

à Nadia Boulanger

PASTORALE

G.-O. Flûte harmonique
Récit. Viole de gambe et Cor de nuit
Positif. Cromorne ou Clarinette
Péd. Basses douces 8, 16.

ROGER-DUCASSE
1873–1954

G.O. accouplé au Récit
ajoutez flûte 8p.
G.O.
p
découplez G.O.
R
p
enlevez flûte 8
rall.
rall.
rall.

1er Mouvt
p subito
p subito
acc. R.
découplez
Très tranquille
pp
ajoutez flûte 8
pp
ajoutez flûte 4
enlevez flûte 4

Très souple
Pos.
p
p
enlevez le 16 P.
G. O.
p
p subito
p subito
R
p
p
G. O.
ajoutez quelques jeux de fonds
16 P.

p
p
(16 P.)
tir. G.O.
rall.
p subito
a tempo
p
G.O. acc. au R.
G.O. ajoutez Montre
découplez R.
R.
p
f
Très souple:
pp
pp
ôtez tir. G.O.

109

pp

tir. **R.**

pp

ajoutez flûte 4

scherzando

pp

G. O. et **R.** = Les 2 claviers dans la même sonorité

pp

110

ajoutez quelques fonds

G. O. ajoutez Montre

ff (anches 8)

R. ajoutez trompette boîte fermée

G.O.

ajoutez prestant

toujours au R. flûte 8 Solo

pp

Pos.

un peu en dehors

p

enlevez les anches

Très expressif.

(8 Pieds)

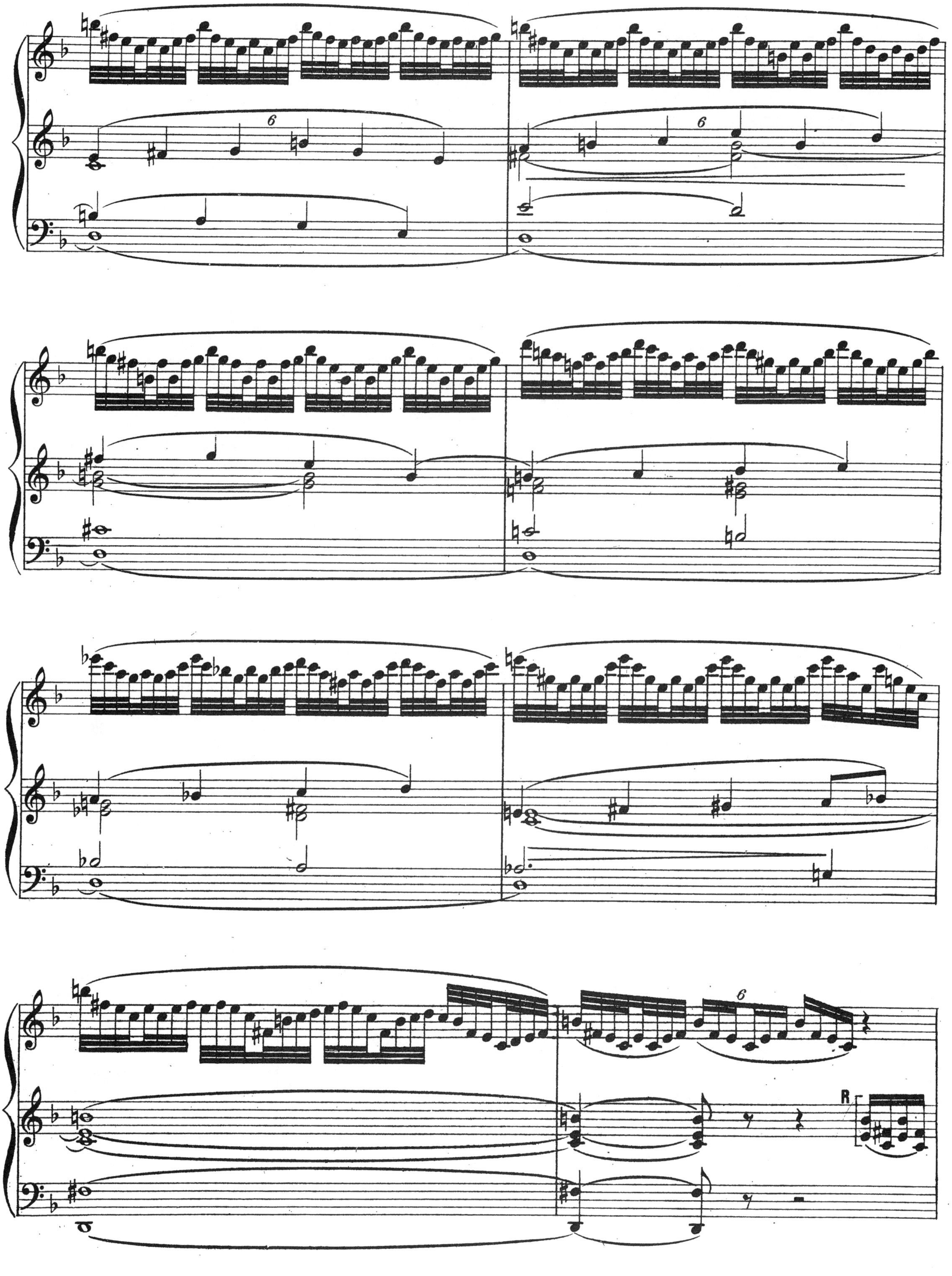

6
6
6
R

G. O. flûte solo
R. ajoutez viole de gambe
ajoutez nasard
Un peu de Mouvement
Pos.
ajoutez tous les fonds R.
R
Pos.
tir. G. O.
G. O. fonds
(16 P.)

G. O.
acc. R.
ajoutez fonds 8 et 16
anches R. boîte fermée
p
ajoutez peu à peu anches G. O. et Ped. jusqu'aux fff
tir. R.
cresc.
cresc. f

16 p.
ôtez 16 p.
ôtez anches Ped.
Aussi vite que possible
ajoutez 16 p.
G. O.
R. acc. Pos. fonds et anches
R
tir. Pos.
Anches Ped.

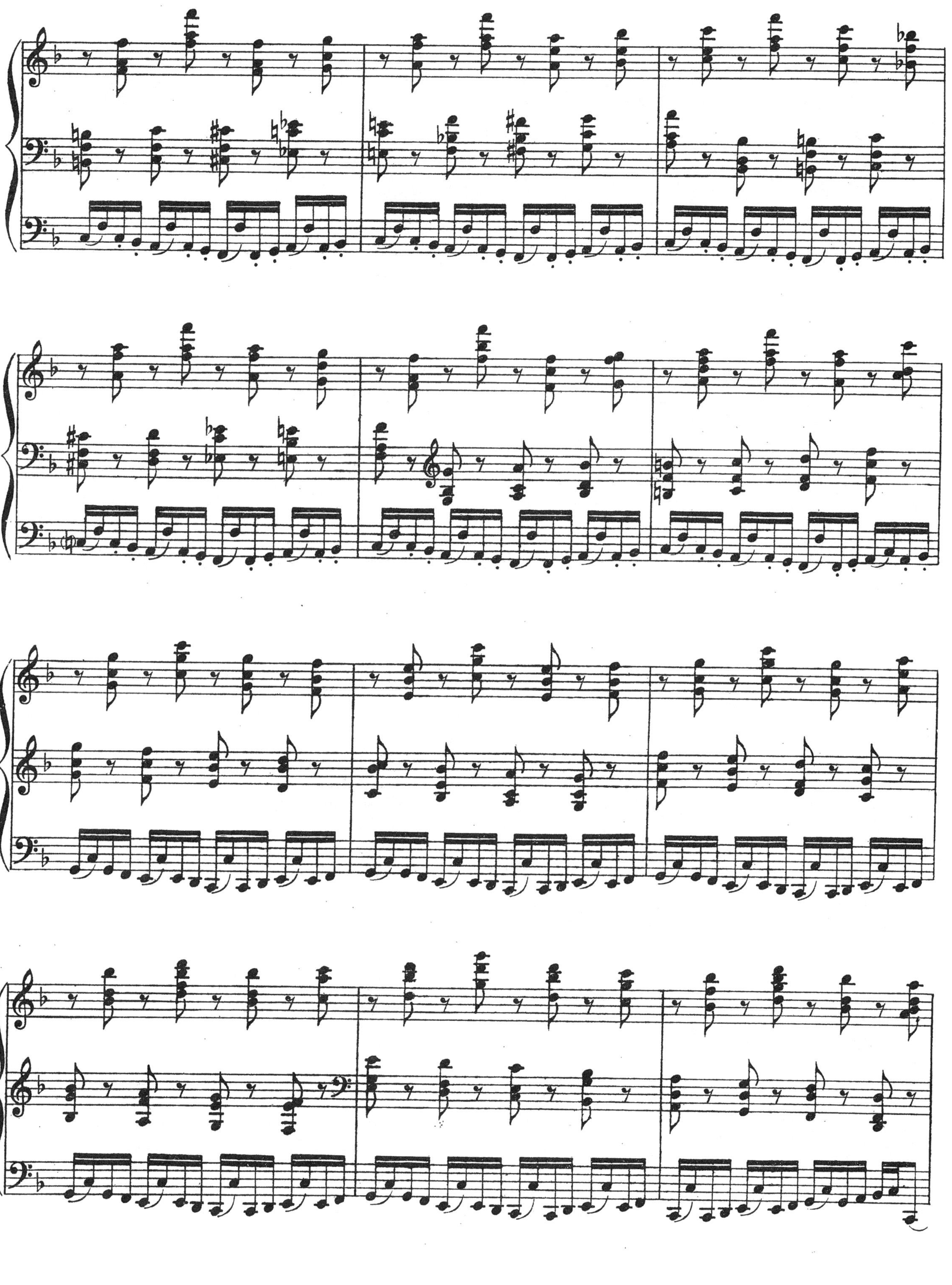

3 claviers acc.
G. O.
sempre ff
fff
élargi
R.
Mouvement Initial
Viole de gambe
ppp
et voix céleste
sans tir. Basses douces 8 et 16
Préparez G.O. flûte 8 solo
Pos. Bourdon et Salicional
pp

Très expressif

Un peu en dehors, mais sans anches

Ralentissez jusqu'au Mouvement initial

G.O.

Récit

rall. - - - -

Adagiosissimo

R.

Pos.

Récit

Mouvement initial

Flûte = 4 Pieds solo

Pos.

sans ralentir

TROIS PIÈCES

à ma femme

I. Pièce solennelle

Fonds et Anches 8 – 4 – 2 à tous les claviers.
PÉDALE: Fonds et Anches 8 – 4
Claviers accouplés. Tirasses.

JACQUES IBERT
1890–1962

(REC.)- Flûtes et Bourdons 8-4
pp
(G. P. R.)
ff
(REC.)
m.d.
pp
(G. P. R.)
ff
m.d.
(REC.)
et Anches
mf
(P. R.)
f
(REC.)
sans Anches
p
(P. R.)
Un peu retenu
pp
sf
(REC.)
boîte fermée

(REC.) Flûte et Bourdon de 8
pp
(POS.) sans Anches
(soutenu)
Ajouter Clarin.
più f
p
Fonds doux 16 et 8
m.d
più p
Enlever Clarin.
Un peu retenu

a Tempo
p
(REC.) très fondu
(P. R.)
mf
poco cresc.
Ajouter Anches REC. (boîte fermée)
toujours cresc.
Tirasses
mf
Anches POS.
f

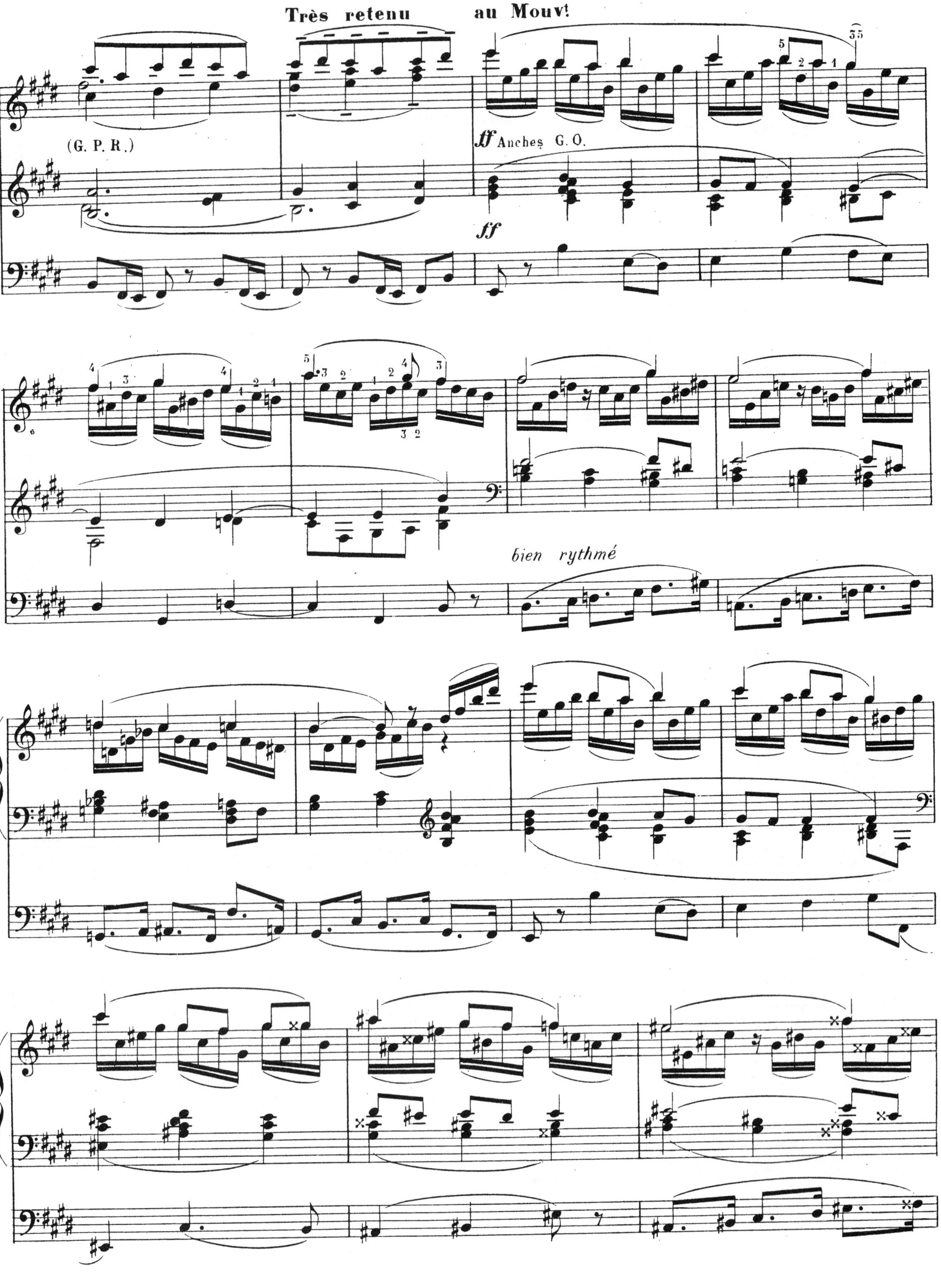
Très retenu
au Mouv!
(G. P. R.)
ff Anches G. O.
ff
bien rythmé

Élargissez beaucoup
16 Pieds G.O.
Ajouter peu à peu tous les 16 pieds
Au mouv!
fff
sans ralentir
Anches Ped.
Joyeux
toujours ff

à MARCEL DUPRÉ

II. Musette

Fonds et Anches 8 – 4 – 2 à tous les claviers.
PÉDALE: Fonds doux de 8
Anches préparées.

Au mouv!
Ajouter V. H.
pp (REC)
(POS.)
(G.O.) mf
Ajouter Bourdon de 16 au G.O.
(G.P.R.) f et joyeux
Ajouter 16 et 4 pieds
cresc. e
f
stringendo
Anches REC.
f
sempre string.

ritard.
Au mouv!
Anches POS
Au mouv!
Tirasses
ff
f
Enlever Anches POS.
Enlever Anches REC.
dimin.
Enlever Tirasses
Ralentissez
(POS.)
Enlever Bourdon 16
au G. O.
Enlever jeux de
4 et 16
pp

1.er Mouv! (Rec. boite fermée)
p
(P. R.)
(G.O.)
mf
G. P. R.
cresc.
*Anches REC.
*Anches POS.
Tirasses

Ajouter fonds 16 pieds
f
poco stretto
sempre stretto
f
sans ralentir
f

à Mademoiselle NADIA BOULANGER

III. Fugue

Fonds de 8 – 4 – 2 - à tous les claviers
PÉDALE: Fonds 8 – 4. Tirasses doux de 8
Claviers accouplés.

Modéré

mp espress.

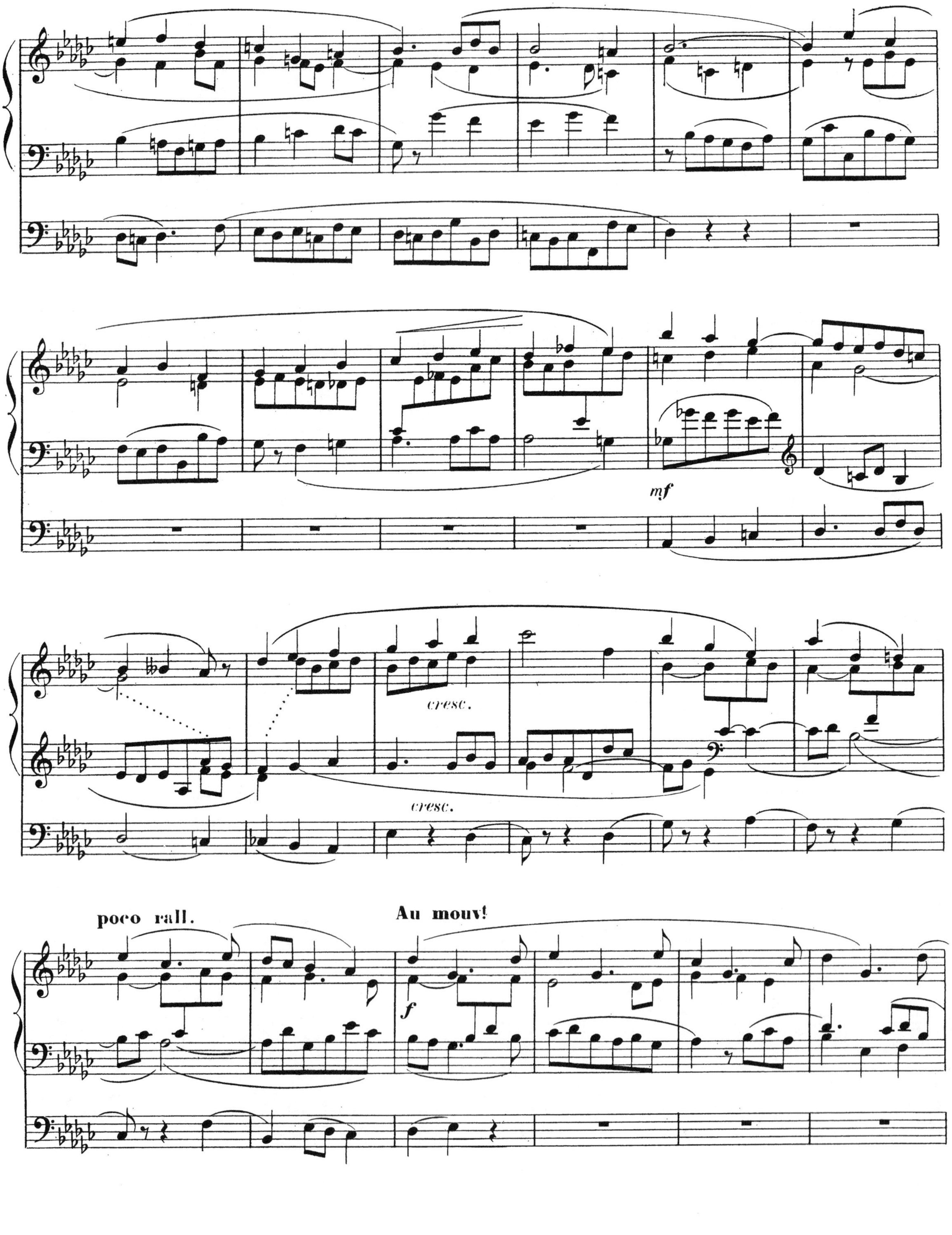
mf
cresc.
cresc.
poco rall.
Au mouvt
f

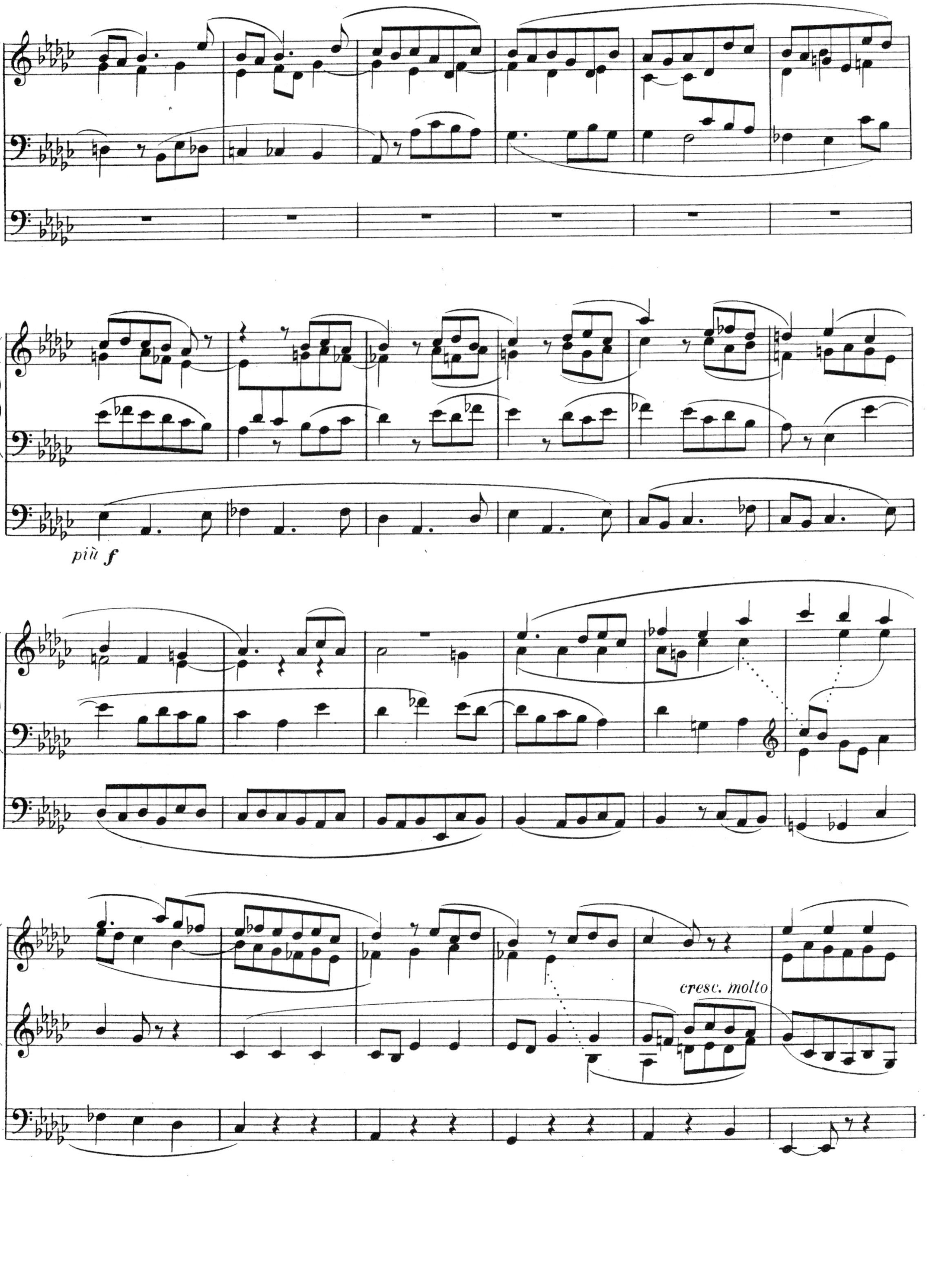
più f
cresc. molto

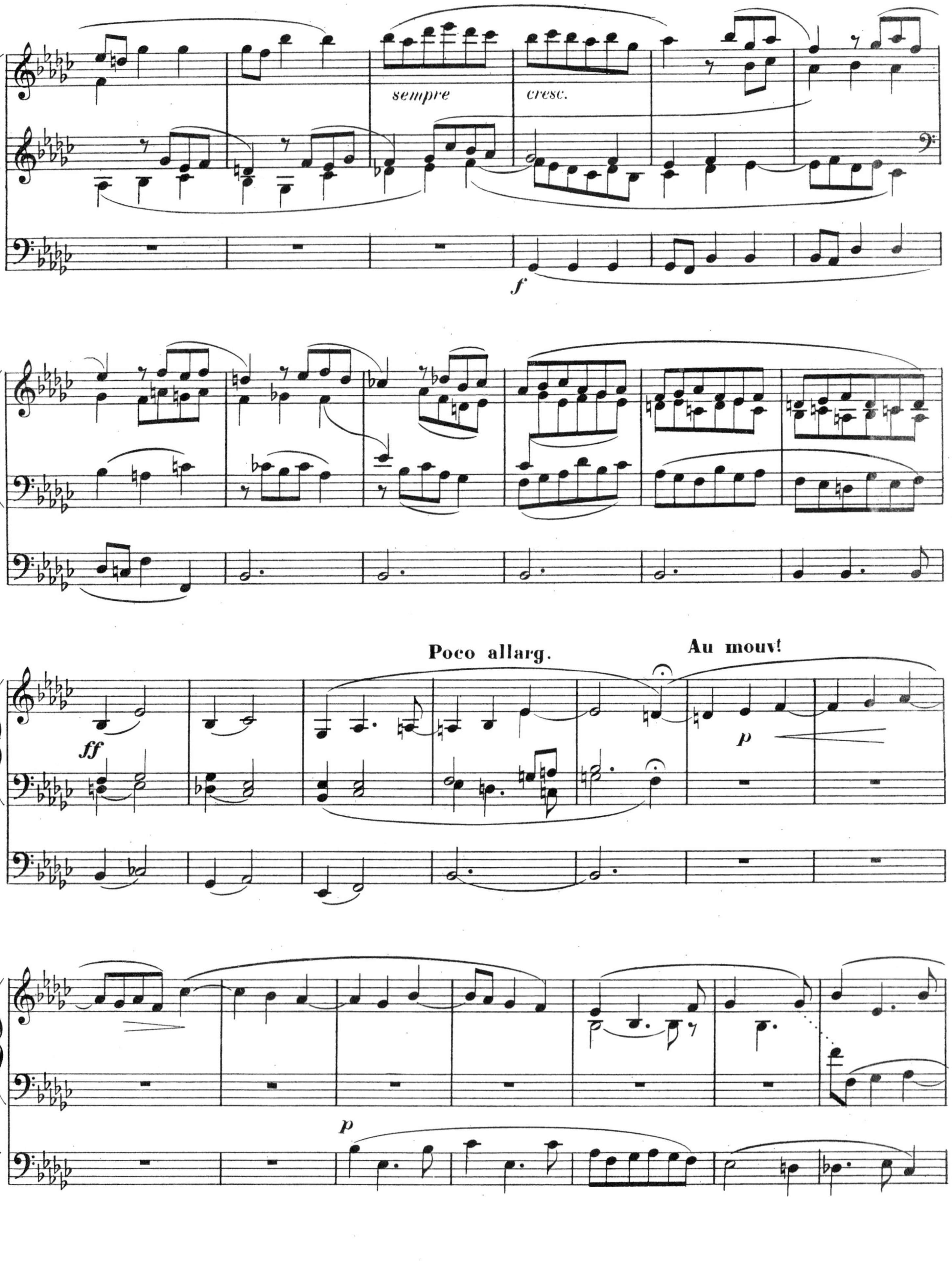
sempre
cresc.
f
ff
Poco allarg.
Au mouv!
p
p

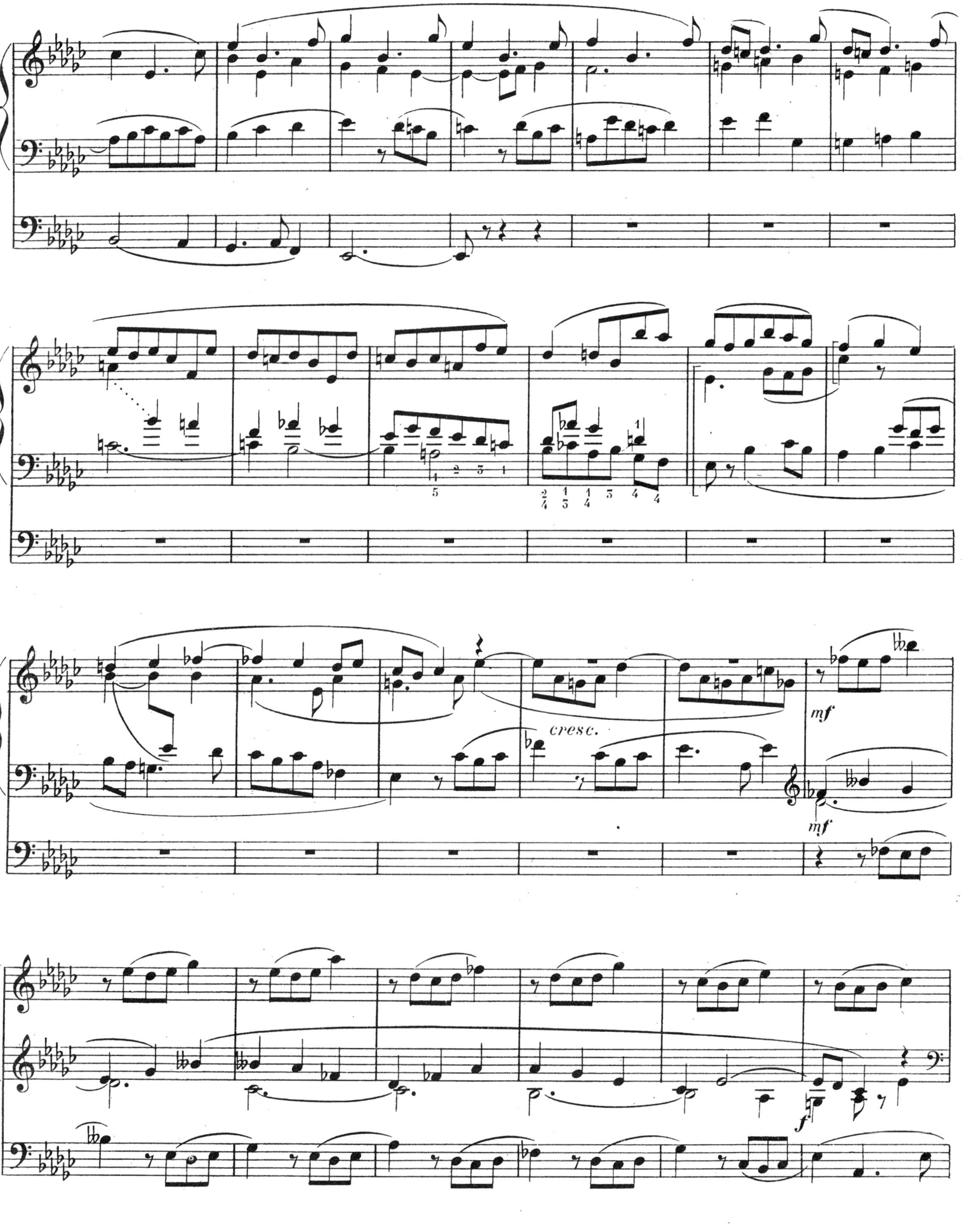
cresc.
mf
mf
f

f
ritard.
sff
Un peu plus lent
sff
sff
Poco allarg.
Au mouvt
ff
ff

TWO PIECES

A Robert Charles Martin

I. FUGUE

Rescored by LYNNWOOD FARNAM

ARTHUR HONEGGER
1892–1955

G. Orgue
p
19
cresc.
22
dim.
p
cresc.
26
ff
+4' coupler
mf
add Ped. Open Wood 16'

Tempo I
tranquillo
p
dim.
ritard.
Récit.
pp
Gamba only
Horn only
8' only
pp
35
*
add 16 ft.
40
44
ritard.
pp
Paris, September 1917

II.
CHORAL

A Andrée Vaurabourg

Lento sostenuto. (♩ = 48)

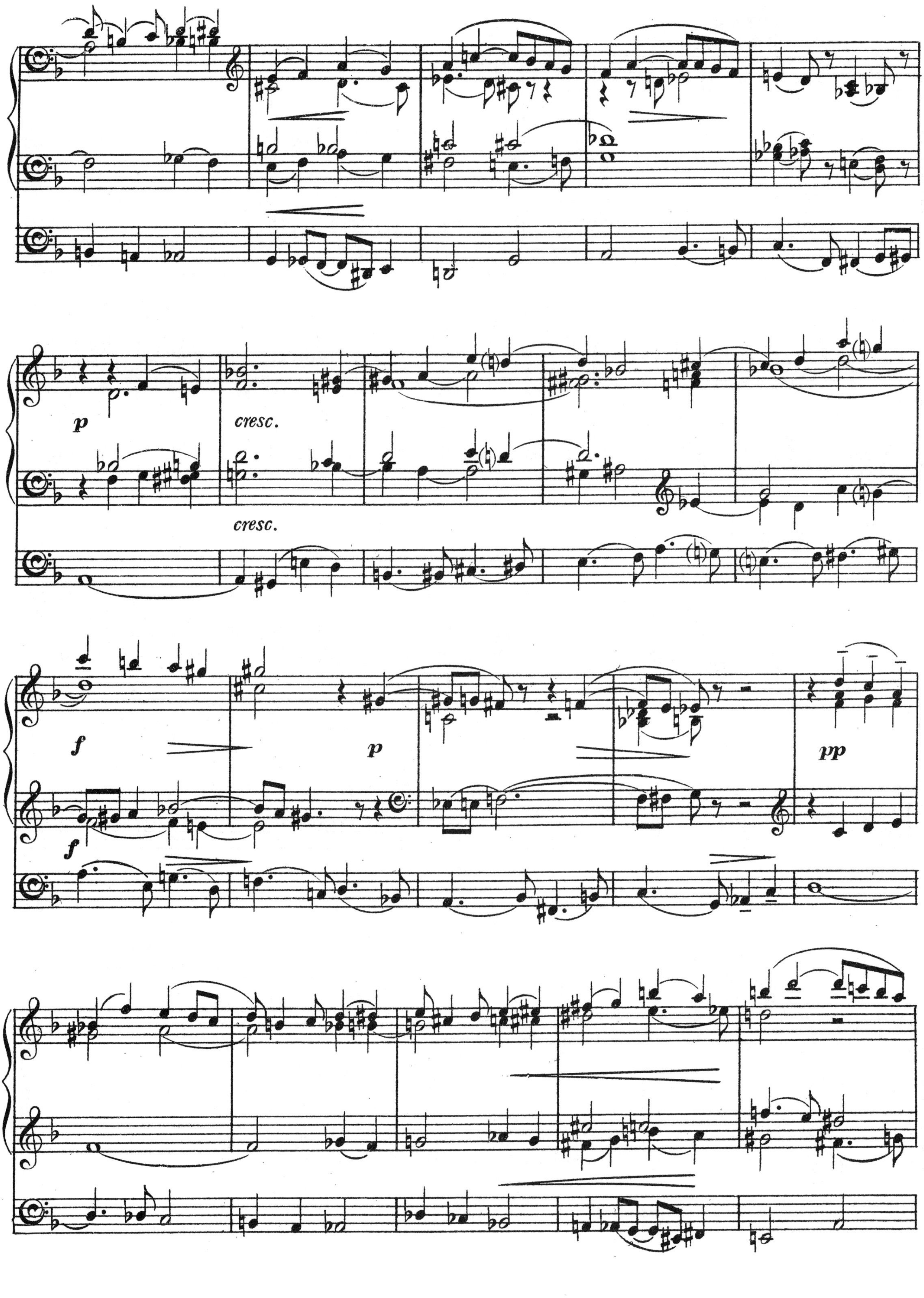
p
cresc.
cresc.
f
p
f
pp

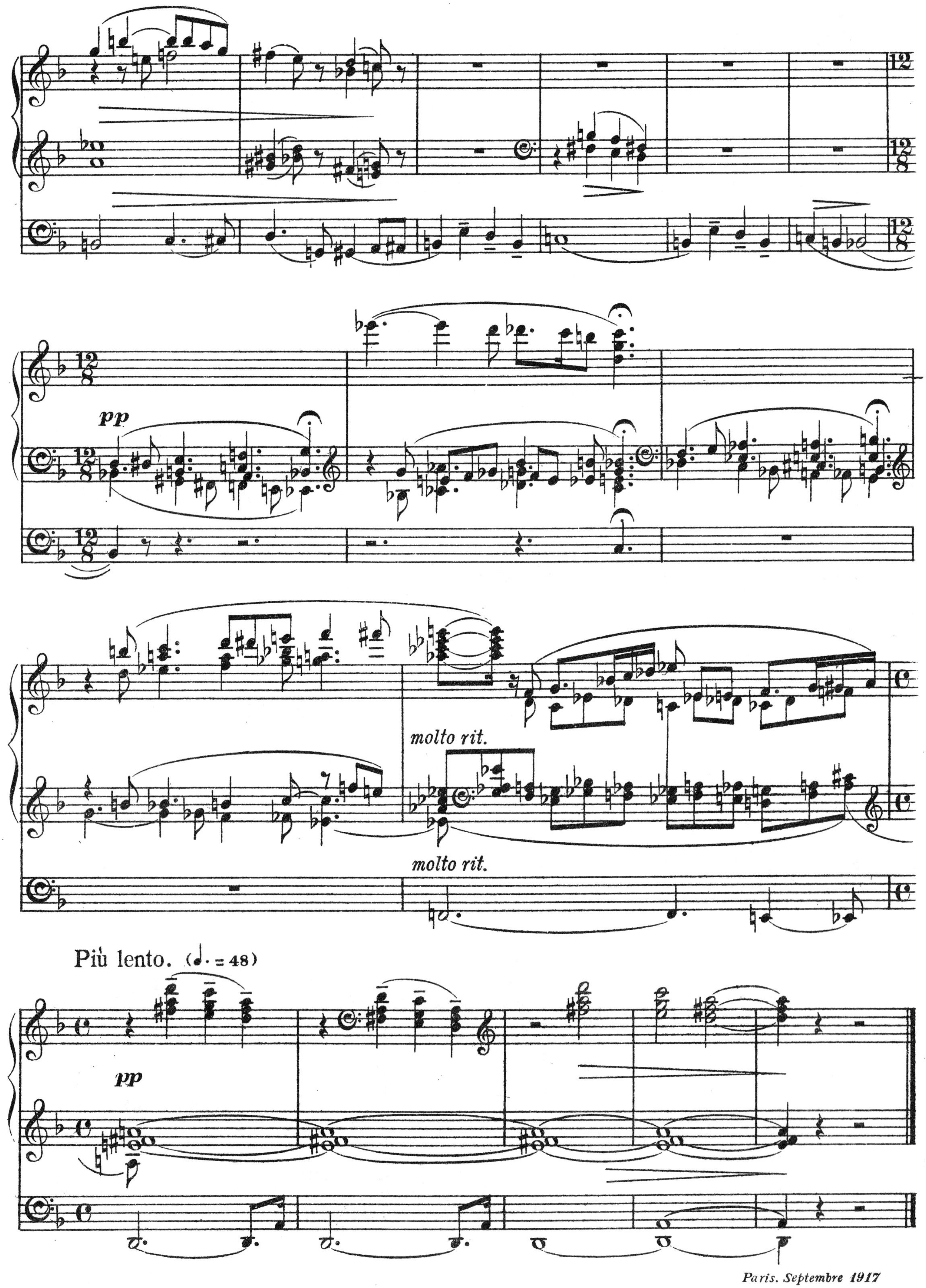
pp
molto rit.
molto rit.
Più lento. (♩. = 48)
pp
Paris. Septembre 1917

INDEX

ALPHABETICAL BY COMPOSER

BOËLLMANN, Léon	Suite Gothique, Op. 25	
	I. Introduction – Choral	54
	II. Menuet gothique	56
	III. Prière à Notre-Dame	61
	IV. Toccata	65
BOËLY, Alexandre-P.-F.	Style Moderne, Op. 43, No. 8	2
CHAUSSON, Ernest	Les Vêpres des Vierges, Op. 31	
	I. Hæc est virgo Sapiens et una	38
	II. Hæc est virgo Sapiens, quam Dominus	38
	III. Hæ est quæ nescivit	39
	IV. Veni electa mea	39
	V. Ista est speciosa	39
	VI. Veni sponsa Christi	40
	VII. Prudentes Virgines	42
	VIII. Veni sponsa Christi	47
	AUTRES ANTIENNES BRÈVES POUR LE MAGNIFICAT	
	I. [Modéré]	51
	II. [Sans lenteur]	52
	III. [Mouv^t. de Choral]	53
GIGOUT, Eugène	Grand Chœur dialogué	21
GOUNOD, Charles	Marche Solennelle	6
GUILMANT, Alexandre	Marche sur un Thème de Hændel, Op. 15, No. 2	28
HONEGGER, Arthur	Two Pieces	
	I. Fugue	135
	II. Choral	138
IBERT, Jacques	Trois Pièces	118
MASSENET, Jules	Prélude en Ut Majeur	36
PIERNÉ, Gabriel	Trois Pièces, Op. 29	
	I. Prélude	75
	II. Cantilène	80
	III. Scherzando de Concert	84
ROGER-DUCASSE, Jean	Pastorale	104
SAINT-SAËNS, Camille	Fantaisie in E-flat	12
SATIE, Erik	Messe des Pauvres	
	I. [Kyrie eleison]	94
	II. Dixit domine	98
	III. Prière des Orgues	99
	IV. Commune qui mundi nefas	101
	V. Chant Ecclésiastique	102
	VI. Prière pour les voyageurs et les marins en danger de mort, à la très bonne et très august Vierge Marie, mère de Jésus.	102
	VII. Prière pour le salut de mon âme	103

Dover Orchestral Scores

Bach, Johann Sebastian, COMPLETE CONCERTI FOR SOLO KEYBOARD AND ORCHESTRA IN FULL SCORE. Bach's seven complete concerti for solo keyboard and orchestra in full score from the authoritative Bach-Gesellschaft edition. 206pp. 9 x 12. 24929-8

Bach, Johann Sebastian, THE SIX BRANDENBURG CONCERTOS AND THE FOUR ORCHESTRAL SUITES IN FULL SCORE. Complete standard Bach-Gesellschaft editions in large, clear format. Study score. 273pp. 9 x 12. 23376-6

Bach, Johann Sebastian, THE THREE VIOLIN CONCERTI IN FULL SCORE. Concerto in A Minor, BWV 1041; Concerto in E Major, BWV 1042; and Concerto for Two Violins in D Minor, BWV 1043. Bach-Gesellschaft editions. 64pp. 9⅜ x 12¼. 25124-1

Beethoven, Ludwig van, COMPLETE PIANO CONCERTOS IN FULL SCORE. Complete scores of five great Beethoven piano concertos, with all cadenzas as he wrote them, reproduced from authoritative Breitkopf & Härtel edition. New Table of Contents. 384pp. 9⅜ x 12¼. 24563-2

Beethoven, Ludwig van, SIX GREAT OVERTURES IN FULL SCORE. Six staples of the orchestral repertoire from authoritative Breitkopf & Härtel edition. *Leonore Overtures,* Nos. 1–3; Overtures to *Coriolanus, Egmont, Fidelio.* 288pp. 9 x 12. 24789-9

Beethoven, Ludwig van, SYMPHONIES NOS. 1, 2, 3, AND 4 IN FULL SCORE. Republication of H. Litolff edition. 272pp. 9 x 12. 26033-X

Beethoven, Ludwig van, SYMPHONIES NOS. 5, 6 AND 7 IN FULL SCORE, Ludwig van Beethoven. Republication of H. Litolff edition. 272pp. 9 x 12. 26034-8

Beethoven, Ludwig van, SYMPHONIES NOS. 8 AND 9 IN FULL SCORE. Republication of H. Litolff edition. 256pp. 9 x 12. 26035-6

Beethoven, Ludwig van; Mendelssohn, Felix; and Tchaikovsky, Peter Ilyitch, GREAT ROMANTIC VIOLIN CONCERTI IN FULL SCORE. The Beethoven Op. 61, Mendelssohn Op. 64 and Tchaikovsky Op. 35 concertos reprinted from Breitkopf & Härtel editions. 224pp. 9 x 12. 24989-1

Brahms, Johannes, COMPLETE CONCERTI IN FULL SCORE. Piano Concertos Nos. 1 and 2; Violin Concerto, Op. 77; Concerto for Violin and Cello, Op. 102. Definitive Breitkopf & Härtel edition. 352pp. 9⅜ x 12¼. 24170-X

Brahms, Johannes, COMPLETE SYMPHONIES. Full orchestral scores in one volume. No. 1 in C Minor, Op. 68; No. 2 in D Major, Op. 73; No. 3 in F Major, Op. 90; and No. 4 in E Minor, Op. 98. Reproduced from definitive Vienna Gesellschaft der Musikfreunde edition. Study score. 344pp. 9 x 12. 23053-8

Brahms, Johannes, THREE ORCHESTRAL WORKS IN FULL SCORE: Academic Festival Overture, Tragic Overture and Variations on a Theme by Joseph Haydn. Reproduced from the authoritative Breitkopf & Härtel edition three of Brahms's great orchestral favorites. Editor's commentary in German and English. 112pp. 9⅜ x 12¼. 24637-X

Chopin, Frédéric, THE PIANO CONCERTOS IN FULL SCORE. The authoritative Breitkopf & Härtel full-score edition in one volume; Piano Concertos No. 1 in E Minor and No. 2 in F Minor. 176pp. 9 x 12. 25835-1

Corelli, Arcangelo, COMPLETE CONCERTI GROSSI IN FULL SCORE. All 12 concerti in the famous late nineteenth-century edition prepared by violinist Joseph Joachim and musicologist Friedrich Chrysander. 240pp. 8⅜ x 11¼. 25606-5

Debussy, Claude, THREE GREAT ORCHESTRAL WORKS IN FULL SCORE. Three of the Impressionist's most-recorded, most-performed favorites: *Prélude à l'Après-midi d'un Faune, Nocturnes,* and *La Mer.* Reprinted from early French editions. 279pp. 9 x 12. 24441-5

Dvořák, Antonín, SERENADE NO. 1, OP. 22, AND SERENADE NO. 2, OP. 44, IN FULL SCORE. Two works typified by elegance of form, intense harmony, rhythmic variety, and uninhibited emotionalism. 96pp. 9 x 12. 41895-2

Dvořák, Antonín, SYMPHONY NO. 8 IN G MAJOR, OP. 88, SYMPHONY NO. 9 IN E MINOR, OP. 95 ("NEW WORLD") IN FULL SCORE. Two celebrated symphonies by the great Czech composer, the Eighth and the immensely popular Ninth, "From the New World," in one volume. 272pp. 9 x 12. 24749-X

Elgar, Edward, CELLO CONCERTO IN E MINOR, OP. 85, IN FULL SCORE. A tour de force for any cellist, this frequently performed work is widely regarded as an elegy for a lost world. Melodic and evocative, it exhibits a remarkable scope, ranging from tragic passion to buoyant optimism. Reproduced from an authoritative source. 112pp. 8⅜ x 11. 41896-0

Franck, César, SYMPHONY IN D MINOR IN FULL SCORE. Superb, authoritative edition of Franck's only symphony, an often-performed and recorded masterwork of late French romantic style. 160pp. 9 x 12. 25373-2

Handel, George Frideric, COMPLETE CONCERTI GROSSI IN FULL SCORE. Monumental Opus 6 Concerti Grossi, Opus 3 and "Alexander's Feast" Concerti Grossi—19 in all—reproduced from the most authoritative edition. 258pp. 9⅜ x 12¼. 24187-4

Handel, George Frideric, GREAT ORGAN CONCERTI, OPP. 4 & 7, IN FULL SCORE. 12 organ concerti composed by the great Baroque master are reproduced in full score from the Deutsche Handelgesellschaft edition. 138pp. 9⅜ x 12¼. 24462-8

Handel, George Frideric, WATER MUSIC AND MUSIC FOR THE ROYAL FIREWORKS IN FULL SCORE. Full scores of two of the most popular Baroque orchestral works performed today—reprinted from the definitive Deutsche Handelgesellschaft edition. Total of 96pp. 8⅛ x 11. 25070-9

Haydn, Joseph, SYMPHONIES 88–92 IN FULL SCORE: The Haydn Society Edition. Full score of symphonies Nos. 88 through 92. Large, readable noteheads, ample margins for fingerings, etc., and extensive Editor's Commentary. 304pp. 9 x 12. (Available in U.S. only) 24445-8

Liszt, Franz, THE PIANO CONCERTI IN FULL SCORE. Here in one volume are Piano Concerto No. 1 in E-flat Major and Piano Concerto No. 2 in A Major—among the most studied, recorded, and performed of all works for piano and orchestra. 144pp. 9 x 12. 25221-3

Mahler, Gustav, DAS LIED VON DER ERDE IN FULL SCORE. Mahler's masterpiece, a fusion of song and symphony, reprinted from the original 1912 Universal Edition. English translations of song texts. 160pp. 9 x 12. 25657-X

Mahler, Gustav, SYMPHONIES NOS. 1 AND 2 IN FULL SCORE. Unabridged, authoritative Austrian editions of Symphony No. 1 in D Major ("Titan") and Symphony No. 2 in C Minor ("Resurrection"). 384pp. 8⅛ x 11. 25473-9

Mahler, Gustav, SYMPHONIES NOS. 3 AND 4 IN FULL SCORE. Two brilliantly contrasting masterworks—one scored for a massive ensemble, the other for small orchestra and soloist—reprinted from authoritative Viennese editions. 368pp. 9⅜ x 12¼. 26166-2

Available from your music dealer or write for free Music Catalog to
Dover Publications, Inc., Dept. MUBI, 31 East 2nd Street, Mineola, NY 11501
*Visit us online at **www.doverpublications.com***

Dover Piano and Keyboard Editions

Albeniz, Isaac, IBERIA AND ESPAÑA: Two Complete Works for Solo Piano. Spanish composer's greatest piano works in authoritative editions. Includes the popular "Tango." 192pp. 9 x 12. 25367-8

Bach, Carl Philipp Emanuel, GREAT KEYBOARD SONATAS. Comprehensive two-volume edition contains 51 sonatas by second, most prestigious son of Johann Sebastian Bach. Originality, rich harmony, delicate workmanship. Authoritative French edition. Total of 384pp. 8⅜ x 11¼.
Series I 24853-4
Series II 24854-2

Bach, Johann Sebastian, COMPLETE KEYBOARD TRANSCRIPTIONS OF CONCERTOS BY BAROQUE COMPOSERS. Sixteen concertos by Vivaldi, Telemann and others, transcribed for solo keyboard instruments. Bach-Gesellschaft edition. 128pp. 9⅜ x 12¼. 25529-8

Bach, Johann Sebastian, COMPLETE PRELUDES AND FUGUES FOR ORGAN. All 25 of Bach's complete sets of preludes and fugues (i.e. compositions written as pairs), from the authoritative Bach-Gesellschaft edition. 168pp. 8⅜ x 11. 24816-X

Bach, Johann Sebastian, ITALIAN CONCERTO, CHROMATIC FANTASIA AND FUGUE AND OTHER WORKS FOR KEYBOARD. Sixteen of Bach's best-known, most-performed and most-recorded works for the keyboard, reproduced from the authoritative Bach-Gesellschaft edition. 112pp. 9 x 12. 25387-2

Bach, Johann Sebastian, KEYBOARD MUSIC. Bach-Gesellschaft edition. For harpsichord, piano, other keyboard instruments. English Suites, French Suites, Six Partitas, Goldberg Variations, Two-Part Inventions, Three-Part Sinfonias. 312pp. 8⅛ x 11. 22360-4

Bach, Johann Sebastian, ORGAN MUSIC. Bach-Gesellschaft edition. 93 works. 6 Trio Sonatas, German Organ Mass, Orgelbüchlein, Six Schubler Chorales, 18 Choral Preludes. 357pp. 8⅛ x 11. 22359-0

Bach, Johann Sebastian, TOCCATAS, FANTASIAS, PASSACAGLIA AND OTHER WORKS FOR ORGAN. Over 20 best-loved works including Toccata and Fugue in D Minor, BWV 565; Passacaglia and Fugue in C Minor, BWV 582, many more. Bach-Gesellschaft edition. 176pp. 9 x 12. 25403-8

Bach, Johann Sebastian, TWO- AND THREE-PART INVENTIONS. Reproduction of original autograph ms. Edited by Eric Simon. 62pp. 8⅛ x 11. 21982-8

Bach, Johann Sebastian, THE WELL-TEMPERED CLAVIER: Books I and II, Complete. All 48 preludes and fugues in all major and minor keys. Authoritative Bach-Gesellschaft edition. Explanation of ornaments in English, tempo indications, music corrections. 208pp. 9⅜ x 12¼. 24532-2

Bartók, Béla, PIANO MUSIC OF BÉLA BARTÓK, Series I. New, definitive Archive Edition incorporating composer's corrections. Includes *Funeral March* from *Kossuth, Fourteen Bagatelles,* Bartók's break to modernism. 167pp. 9 x 12. (Available in U.S. only) 24108-4

Bartók, Béla, PIANO MUSIC OF BÉLA BARTÓK, Series II. Second in the Archive Edition incorporating composer's corrections. 85 short pieces *For Children, Two Elegies, Two Romanian Dances,* etc. 192pp. 9 x 12. (Available in U.S. only) 24109-2

Beethoven, Ludwig van, BAGATELLES, RONDOS AND OTHER SHORTER WORKS FOR PIANO. Most popular and most performed shorter works, including Rondo a capriccio in G and Andante in F. Breitkopf & Härtel edition. 128pp. 9⅜ x 12¼. 25392-9

Beethoven, Ludwig van, COMPLETE PIANO SONATAS. All sonatas in fine Schenker edition, with fingering, analytical material. One of best modern editions. 615pp. 9 x 12. Two-vol. set. 23134-8, 23135-6

Beethoven, Ludwig van, COMPLETE VARIATIONS FOR SOLO PIANO, Ludwig van Beethoven. Contains all 21 sets of Beethoven's piano variations, including the extremely popular *Diabelli Variations, Op. 120.* 240pp. 9⅜ x 12¼. 25188-8

Blesh, Rudi (ed.), CLASSIC PIANO RAGS. Best ragtime music (1897–1922) by Scott Joplin, James Scott, Joseph F. Lamb, Tom Turpin, nine others. 364pp. 9 x 12. Introduction by Blesh. 20469-3

Brahms, Johannes, COMPLETE SHORTER WORKS FOR SOLO PIANO. All solo music not in other two volumes. Waltzes, Scherzo in E Flat Minor, Eight Pieces, Rhapsodies, Fantasies, Intermezzi, etc. Vienna Gesellschaft der Musikfreunde. 180pp. 9 x 12. 22651-4

Brahms, Johannes, COMPLETE SONATAS AND VARIATIONS FOR SOLO PIANO. All sonatas, five variations on themes from Schumann, Paganini, Handel, etc. Vienna Gesellschaft der Musikfreunde edition. 178pp. 9 x 12. 22650-6

Brahms, Johannes, COMPLETE TRANSCRIPTIONS, CADENZAS AND EXERCISES FOR SOLO PIANO. Vienna Gesellschaft der Musikfreunde edition, vol. 15. Studies after Chopin, Weber, Bach; gigues, sarabandes; 10 Hungarian dances, etc. 178pp. 9 x 12. 22652-2

Buxtehude, Dietrich, ORGAN WORKS. Complete organ works of extremely influential pre-Bach composer. Toccatas, preludes, chorales, more. Definitive Breitkopf & Härtel edition. 320pp. 8⅜ x 11¼. (Available in U.S. only) 25682-0

Byrd, William, MY LADY NEVELLS BOOKE OF VIRGINAL MUSIC. 42 compositions in modern notation from 1591 ms. For any keyboard instrument. 245pp. 8⅛ x 11. 22246-2

Chopin, Frédéric, COMPLETE BALLADES, IMPROMPTUS AND SONATAS. The four Ballades, four Impromptus and three Sonatas. Authoritative Mikuli edition. 192pp. 9 x 12. 24164-5

Chopin, Frédéric, COMPLETE MAZURKAS, Frédéric Chopin. 51 best-loved compositions, reproduced directly from the authoritative Kistner edition edited by Carl Mikuli. 160pp. 9 x 12. 25548-4

Chopin, Frédéric, COMPLETE PRELUDES AND ETUDES FOR SOLO PIANO. All 25 Preludes and all 27 Etudes by greatest piano music composer. Authoritative Mikuli edition. 192pp. 9 x 12. 24052-5

Chopin, Frédéric, FANTASY IN F MINOR, BARCAROLLE, BERCEUSE AND OTHER WORKS FOR SOLO PIANO. 15 works, including one of the greatest of the Romantic period, the Fantasy in F Minor, Op. 49, reprinted from the authoritative German edition prepared by Chopin's student, Carl Mikuli. 224pp. 8⅜ x 11¼. 25950-1

Chopin, Frédéric, NOCTURNES AND POLONAISES. 20 *Nocturnes* and 11 *Polonaises* reproduced from the authoritative Mikuli edition for pianists, students, and musicologists. Commentary. 224pp. 9 x 12. 24564-0

Chopin, Frédéric, WALTZES AND SCHERZOS. All of the Scherzos and nearly all (20) of the Waltzes from the authoritative Mikuli edition. Editorial commentary. 160pp. 9 x 12. 24316-8

Cofone, Charles J. F. (ed.), ELIZABETH ROGERS HIR VIRGINALL BOOKE. All 112 pieces from noted 1656 manuscript, most never before published. Composers include Thomas Brewer, William Byrd, Orlando Gibbons, etc. Calligraphy by editor. 125pp. 9 x 12. 23138-0

Available from your music dealer or write for free Music Catalog to
Dover Publications, Inc., Dept. MUBI, 31 East 2nd Street, Mineola, NY 11501
Visit us online at www.doverpublications.com

Dover Piano and Keyboard Editions

Couperin, François, KEYBOARD WORKS/Series One: Ordres I–XIII; Series Two: Ordres XIV–XXVII and Miscellaneous Pieces. Over 200 pieces. Reproduced directly from edition prepared by Johannes Brahms and Friedrich Chrysander. Total of 496pp. 8⅛ x 11.
Series I 25795-9
Series II 25796-7

Debussy, Claude, COMPLETE PRELUDES, Books 1 and 2. 24 evocative works that reveal the essence of Debussy's genius for musical imagery, among them many of the composer's most famous piano compositions. Glossary of French terms. 128pp. 8⅜ x 11¼. 25970-6

Debussy, Claude, DEBUSSY MASTERPIECES FOR SOLO PIANO: 20 Works. From France's most innovative and influential composer–a rich compilation of works that include "Golliwogg's cakewalk," "Engulfed cathedral," "Clair de lune," and 17 others. 128pp. 9 x 12. 42425-1

Debussy, Claude, PIANO MUSIC 1888–1905. Deux Arabesques, Suite Bergamesque, Masques, first series of Images, etc. Nine others, in corrected editions. 175pp. 9⅜ x 12¼. 22771-5

Dvořák, Antonín, HUMORESQUES AND OTHER WORKS FOR SOLO PIANO. Humoresques, Op. 101, complete, Silhouettes, Op. 8, Poetic Tone Pictures, Theme with Variations, Op. 36, 4 Slavonic Dances, more. 160pp. 9 x 12. 28355-0

Fauré, Gabriel, COMPLETE PRELUDES, IMPROMPTUS AND VALSES-CAPRICES. Eighteen elegantly wrought piano works in authoritative editions. Only one-volume collection available. 144pp. 9 x 12. (Not available in France or Germany) 25789-4

Fauré, Gabriel, NOCTURNES AND BARCAROLLES FOR SOLO PIANO. 12 nocturnes and 12 barcarolles reprinted from authoritative French editions. 208pp. 9⅜ x 12¼. (Not available in France or Germany) 27955-3

Feofanov, Dmitry (ed.), RARE MASTERPIECES OF RUSSIAN PIANO MUSIC: Eleven Pieces by Glinka, Balakirev, Glazunov and Others. Glinka's *Prayer*, Balakirev's *Reverie*, Liapunov's *Transcendental Etude*, Op. 11, No. 10, and eight others–full, authoritative scores from Russian texts. 144pp. 9 x 12. 24659-0

Franck, César, ORGAN WORKS. Composer's best-known works for organ, including Six Pieces, Trois Pieces, and Trois Chorals. Oblong format for easy use at keyboard. Authoritative Durand edition. 208pp. 11⅜ x 8¼. 25517-4

Franck, César, SELECTED PIANO COMPOSITIONS, edited by Vincent d'Indy. Outstanding selection of influential French composer's piano works, including early pieces and the two masterpieces–Prelude, Choral and Fugue; and Prelude, Aria and Finale. Ten works in all. 138pp. 9 x 12. 23269-7

Gillespie, John (ed.), NINETEENTH-CENTURY EUROPEAN PIANO MUSIC: Unfamiliar Masterworks. Difficult-to-find etudes, toccatas, polkas, impromptus, waltzes, etc., by Albéniz, Bizet, Chabrier, Fauré, Smetana, Richard Strauss, Wagner and 16 other composers. 62 pieces. 343pp. 9 x 12. (Not available in France or Germany) 23447-9

Gottschalk, Louis M., PIANO MUSIC. 26 pieces (including covers) by early 19th-century American genius. "Bamboula," "The Banjo," other Creole, Negro-based material, through elegant salon music. 301pp. 9¼ x 12. 21683-7

Granados, Enrique, GOYESCAS, SPANISH DANCES AND OTHER WORKS FOR SOLO PIANO. Great Spanish composer's most admired, most performed suites for the piano, in definitive Spanish editions. 176pp. 9 x 12. 25481-X

Grieg, Edvard, COMPLETE LYRIC PIECES FOR PIANO. All 66 pieces from Grieg's ten sets of little mood pictures for piano, favorites of generations of pianists. 224pp. 9⅜ x 12¼. 26176-X

Handel, G. F., KEYBOARD WORKS FOR SOLO INSTRUMENTS. 35 neglected works from Handel's vast oeuvre, originally jotted down as improvisations. Includes Eight Great Suites, others. New sequence. 174pp. 9⅜ x 12¼. 24338-9

Haydn, Joseph, COMPLETE PIANO SONATAS. 52 sonatas reprinted from authoritative Breitkopf & Härtel edition. Extremely clear and readable; ample space for notes, analysis. 464pp. 9⅜ x 12¼.
Vol. I 24726-0
Vol. II 24727-9

Jasen, David A. (ed.), RAGTIME GEMS: Original Sheet Music for 25 Ragtime Classics. Includes original sheet music and covers for 25 rags, including three of Scott Joplin's finest: "Searchlight Rag," "Rose Leaf Rag," and "Fig Leaf Rag." 122pp. 9 x 12. 25248-5

Joplin, Scott, COMPLETE PIANO RAGS. All 38 piano rags by the acknowledged master of the form, reprinted from the publisher's original editions complete with sheet music covers. Introduction by David A. Jasen. 208pp. 9 x 12. 25807-6

Liszt, Franz, ANNÉES DE PÈLERINAGE, COMPLETE. Authoritative Russian edition of piano masterpieces: *Première Année (Suisse): Deuxième Année (Italie)* and *Venezia e Napoli; Troisième Année*, other related pieces. 288pp. 9⅜ x 12¼. 25627-8

Liszt, Franz, BEETHOVEN SYMPHONIES NOS. 6–9 TRANSCRIBED FOR SOLO PIANO. Includes Symphony No. 6 in F major, Op. 68, "Pastorale"; Symphony No. 7 in A major, Op. 92; Symphony No. 8 in F major, Op. 93; and Symphony No. 9 in D minor, Op. 125, "Choral." A memorable tribute from one musical genius to another. 224pp. 9 x 12. 41884-7

Liszt, Franz, COMPLETE ETUDES FOR SOLO PIANO, Series I: Including the Transcendental Etudes, edited by Busoni. Also includes Etude in 12 Exercises, 12 Grandes Etudes and Mazeppa. Breitkopf & Härtel edition. 272pp. 8⅜ x 11¼. 25815-7

Liszt, Franz, COMPLETE ETUDES FOR SOLO PIANO, Series II: Including the Paganini Etudes and Concert Etudes, edited by Busoni. Also includes Morceau de Salon, Ab Irato. Breitkopf & Härtel edition. 192pp. 8⅜ x 11¼. 25816-5

Liszt, Franz, COMPLETE HUNGARIAN RHAPSODIES FOR SOLO PIANO. All 19 Rhapsodies reproduced directly from authoritative Russian edition. All headings, footnotes translated to English. 224pp. 8⅜ x 11¼. 24744-9

Liszt, Franz, MEPHISTO WALTZ AND OTHER WORKS FOR SOLO PIANO. Rapsodie Espagnole, Liebestraüme Nos. 1–3, Valse Oubliée No. 1, Nuages Gris, Polonaises Nos. 1 and 2, Grand Galop Chromatique, more. 192pp. 8⅜ x 11¼. 28147-7

Liszt, Franz, PIANO TRANSCRIPTIONS FROM FRENCH AND ITALIAN OPERAS. Virtuoso transformations of themes by Mozart, Verdi, Bellini, other masters, into unforgettable music for piano. Published in association with American Liszt Society. 247pp. 9 x 12. 24273-0

Liszt, Franz, SONATA IN B MINOR AND OTHER WORKS FOR PIANO. One of Liszt's most frequently performed piano masterpieces, with the six Consolations, ten *Harmonies poetiques et religieuses*, two Ballades and two Legendes. Breitkopf & Härtel edition. 208pp. 8⅜ x 11¼. 26182-4

Maitland, J. Fuller, Squire, W. B. (eds.), THE FITZWILLIAM VIRGINAL BOOK. Famous early 17th-century collection of keyboard music, 300 works by Morley, Byrd, Bull, Gibbons, etc. Modern notation. Total of 938pp. 8⅜ x 11. Two-vol. set. 21068-5, 21069-3

Available from your music dealer or write for free Music Catalog to
Dover Publications, Inc., Dept. MUBI, 31 East 2nd Street, Mineola, NY 11501
Visit us online at www.doverpublications.com

Dover Piano and Keyboard Editions

Mendelssohn, Felix, COMPLETE WORKS FOR PIANOFORTE SOLO. Breitkopf and Härtel edition of Capriccio in F# Minor, Sonata in E Major, Fantasy in F# Minor, Three Caprices, Songs without Words, and 20 other works. Total of 416pp. 9⅜ x 12¼. Two-vol. set. 23136-4, 23137-2

Mozart, Wolfgang Amadeus, MOZART MASTERPIECES: 19 WORKS FOR SOLO PIANO. Superb assortment includes sonatas, fantasies, variations, rondos, minuets, and more. Highlights include "Turkish Rondo," "Sonata in C," and a dozen variations on "Ah, vous dirai-je, Maman" (the familiar tune "Twinkle, Twinkle, Little Star"). Convenient, attractive, inexpensive volume; authoritative sources. 128pp. 9 x 12. 40408-0

Pachelbel, Johann, THE FUGUES ON THE MAGNIFICAT FOR ORGAN OR KEYBOARD. 94 pieces representative of Pachelbel's magnificent contribution to keyboard composition; can be played on the organ, harpsichord or piano. 100pp. 9 x 12. (Available in U.S. only) 25037-7

Phillipp, Isidor (ed.), FRENCH PIANO MUSIC, AN ANTHOLOGY. 44 complete works, 1670–1905, by Lully, Couperin, Rameau, Alkan, Saint-Saëns, Delibes, Bizet, Godard, many others; favorite and lesser-known examples, all top quality. 188pp. 9 x 12. (Not available in France or Germany) 23381-2

Prokofiev, Sergei, PIANO SONATAS NOS. 1–4, OPP. 1, 14, 28, 29. Includes the dramatic Sonata No. 1 in F minor; Sonata No. 2 in D minor, a masterpiece in four movements; Sonata No. 3 in A minor, a brilliant 7-minute score; and Sonata No. 4 in C minor, a three-movement sonata considered vintage Prokofiev. 96pp. 9 x 12. (Available in U.S. only) 42128-7

Rachmaninoff, Serge, COMPLETE PRELUDES AND ETUDES-TABLEAUX. Forty-one of his greatest works for solo piano, including the riveting C Minor, G Minor and B Minor preludes, in authoritative editions. 208pp. 8⅜ x 11¼. 25696-0

Ravel, Maurice, PIANO MASTERPIECES OF MAURICE RAVEL. Handsome affordable treasury; *Pavane pour une infante defunte, jeux d'eau, Sonatine, Miroirs,* more. 128pp. 9 x 12. (Not available in France or Germany) 25137-3

Satie, Erik, GYMNOPÉDIES, GNOSSIENNES AND OTHER WORKS FOR PIANO. The largest Satie collection of piano works yet published, 17 in all, reprinted from the original French editions. 176pp. 9 x 12. (Not available in France or Germany) 25978-1

Satie, Erik, TWENTY SHORT PIECES FOR PIANO (Sports et Divertissements). French master's brilliant thumbnail sketches–verbal and musical–of various outdoor sports and amusements. English translations, 20 illustrations. Rare, limited 1925 edition. 48pp. 12 x 8⅞. (Not available in France or Germany) 24365-6

Scarlatti, Domenico, GREAT KEYBOARD SONATAS, Series I and Series II. 78 of the most popular sonatas reproduced from the G. Ricordi edition edited by Alessandro Longo. Total of 320pp. 8⅝ x 11¼. Series I 24996-4 Series II 25003-2

Schubert, Franz, COMPLETE SONATAS FOR PIANOFORTE SOLO. All 15 sonatas. Breitkopf and Härtel edition. 293pp. 9⅜ x 12¼. 22647-6

Schubert, Franz, DANCES FOR SOLO PIANO. Over 350 waltzes, minuets, landler, ecossaises, and other charming, melodic dance compositions reprinted from the authoritative Breitkopf & Härtel edition. 192pp. 9⅜ x 12¼. 26107-7

Schubert, Franz, SELECTED PIANO WORKS FOR FOUR HANDS. 24 separate pieces (16 most popular titles): Three Military Marches, Lebensstürme, Four Polonaises, Four Ländler, etc. Rehearsal numbers added. 273pp. 9 x 12. 23529-7

Schubert, Franz, SHORTER WORKS FOR PIANOFORTE SOLO. All piano music except Sonatas, Dances, and a few unfinished pieces. Contains Wanderer, Impromptus, Moments Musicals, Variations, Scherzi, etc. Breitkopf and Härtel edition. 199pp. 9⅜ x 12¼. 22648-4

Schumann, Clara (ed.), PIANO MUSIC OF ROBERT SCHUMANN, Series I. Major compositions from the period 1830–39; *Papillons,* Toccata, Grosse Sonate No. 1, *Phantasiestücke, Arabeske, Blumenstück,* and nine other works. Reprinted from Breitkopf & Härtel edition. 274pp. 9⅜ x 12¼. 21459-1

Schumann, Clara (ed.), PIANO MUSIC OF ROBERT SCHUMANN, Series II. Major compositions from period 1838–53; *Humoreske, Novelletten,* Sonate No. 2, 43 *Clavierstücke für die Jugend,* and six other works. Reprinted from Breitkopf & Härtel edition. 272pp. 9⅜ x 12¼. 21461-3

Schumann, Clara (ed.), PIANO MUSIC OF ROBERT SCHUMANN, Series III. All solo music not in other two volumes, including *Symphonic Etudes, Phantaisie,* 13 other choice works. Definitive Breitkopf & Härtel edition. 224pp. 9⅜ x 12¼. 23906-3

Scriabin, Alexander, COMPLETE PIANO SONATAS. All ten of Scriabin's sonatas, reprinted from an authoritative early Russian edition. 256pp. 8⅝ x 11¼. 25850-5

Scriabin, Alexander, THE COMPLETE PRELUDES AND ETUDES FOR PIANOFORTE SOLO. All the preludes and etudes including many perfectly spun miniatures. Edited by K. N. Igumnov and Y. I. Mil'shteyn. 250pp. 9 x 12. 22919-X

Sousa, John Philip, SOUSA'S GREAT MARCHES IN PIANO TRANSCRIPTION. Playing edition includes: "The Stars and Stripes Forever," "King Cotton," "Washington Post," much more. 24 illustrations. 111pp. 9 x 12. 23132-1

Strauss, Johann, Jr., FAVORITE WALTZES, POLKAS AND OTHER DANCES FOR SOLO PIANO. "Blue Danube," "Tales from Vienna Woods," and many other best-known waltzes and other dances. 160pp. 9 x 12. 27851-4

Sweelinck, Jan Pieterszoon, WORKS FOR ORGAN AND KEYBOARD. Nearly all of early Dutch composer's difficult-to-find keyboard works. Chorale variations; toccatas, fantasias; variations on secular, dance tunes. Also, incomplete and/or modified works, plus fantasia by John Bull. 272pp. 9 x 12. 24935-2

Telemann, Georg Philipp, THE 36 FANTASIAS FOR KEYBOARD. Graceful compositions by 18th-century master. 1923 Breslauer edition. 80pp. 8⅛ x 11. 25365-1

Tichenor, Trebor Jay, (ed.), RAGTIME RARITIES. 63 tuneful, rediscovered piano rags by 51 composers (or teams). Does not duplicate selections in *Classic Piano Rags* (Dover, 20469-3). 305pp. 9 x 12. 23157-7

Tichenor, Trebor Jay, (ed.), RAGTIME REDISCOVERIES. 64 unusual rags demonstrate diversity of style, local tradition. Original sheet music. 320pp. 9 x 12. 23776-1

Available from your music dealer or write for ***free*** *Music Catalog to*
Dover Publications, Inc., Dept. MUBI, 31 East 2nd Street, Mineola, NY 11501
Visit us online at ***www.doverpublications.com***

Dover Chamber Music Scores

Bach, Johann Sebastian, COMPLETE SUITES FOR UN-ACCOMPANIED CELLO AND SONATAS FOR VIOLA DA GAMBA. Bach-Gesellschaft edition of the six cello suites (BWV 1007–1012) and three sonatas (BWV 1027–1029), commonly played today on the cello. 112pp. 9⅜ x 12¼. 25641-3

Bach, Johann Sebastian, WORKS FOR VIOLIN. Complete Sonatas and Partitas for Unaccompanied Violin; Six Sonatas for Violin and Clavier. Bach-Gesellschaft edition. 158pp. 9⅜ x 12¼. 23683-8

Beethoven, Ludwig van. COMPLETE SONATAS AND VARIATIONS FOR CELLO AND PIANO. All five sonatas and three sets of variations. Breitkopf & Härtel edition. 176pp. 9⅜ x 12¼. 26441-6

Beethoven, Ludwig van. COMPLETE STRING QUARTETS, Breitkopf & Härtel edition. Six quartets of Opus 18; three quartets of Opus 59; Opera 74, 95, 127, 130, 131, 132, 135 and Grosse Fuge. Study score. 434pp. 9⅜ x 12¼. 22361-2

Beethoven, Ludwig van. COMPLETE VIOLIN SONATAS. All ten sonatas including the "Kreutzer" and "Spring" sonatas in the definitive Breitkopf & Härtel edition. 256pp. 9 x 12. 26277-4

Beethoven, Ludwig van. SIX GREAT PIANO TRIOS IN FULL SCORE. Definitive Breitkopf & Härtel edition of Beethoven's Piano Trios Nos. 1–6 including the "Ghost" and the "Archduke." 224pp. 9⅜ x 12¼. 25398-8

Brahms, Johannes, COMPLETE CHAMBER MUSIC FOR STRINGS AND CLARINET QUINTET. Vienna Gesellschaft der Musikfreunde edition of all quartets, quintets, and sextets without piano. Study edition. 262pp. 8⅜ x 11¼. 21914-3

Brahms, Johannes, COMPLETE PIANO TRIOS. All five piano trios in the definitive Breitkopf & Härtel edition. 288pp. 9 x 12. 25769-X

Brahms, Johannes, COMPLETE SONATAS FOR SOLO INSTRUMENT AND PIANO. All seven sonatas—three for violin, two for cello and two for clarinet (or viola)—reprinted from the authoritative Breitkopf & Härtel edition. 208pp. 9 x 12. 26091-7

Brahms, Johannes, QUINTET AND QUARTETS FOR PIANO AND STRINGS. Full scores of *Quintet in F Minor*, Op. 34; *Quartet in G Minor*, Op. 25; *Quartet in A Major*, Op. 26; *Quartet in C Minor*, Op. 60. Breitkopf & Härtel edition. 298pp. 9 x 12. 24900-X

Debussy, Claude and Ravel, Maurice, STRING QUARTETS BY DEBUSSY AND RAVEL/Claude Debussy: Quartet in G Minor, Op. 10/Maurice Ravel: Quartet in F Major. Authoritative one-volume edition of two influential masterpieces noted for individuality, delicate and subtle beauties. 112pp. 8⅛ x 11. (Not available in France or Germany) 25231-0

Dvořák, Antonín, CHAMBER WORKS FOR PIANO AND STRINGS. Society editions of the F Minor and Dumky piano trios, D Major and E-flat Major piano quartets and A Major piano quintet. 352pp. 8⅛ x 11¼. (Not available in Europe or the United Kingdom) 25663-4

Dvořák, Antonín, FIVE LATE STRING QUARTETS. Treasury of Czech master's finest chamber works: Nos. 10, 11, 12, 13, 14. Reliable Simrock editions. 282pp. 8⅛ x 11. 25135-7

Franck, César, GREAT CHAMBER WORKS. Four great works: Violin Sonata in A Major, Piano Trio in F-sharp Minor, String Quartet in D Major and Piano Quintet in F Minor. From J. Hamelle, Paris and C. F. Peters, Leipzig editions. 248pp. 9⅜ x 12¼. 26546-3

Haydn, Joseph, ELEVEN LATE STRING QUARTETS. Complete reproductions of Op. 74, Nos. 1–3; Op. 76, Nos. 1–6; and Op. 77, Nos. 1 and 2. Definitive Eulenburg edition. Full-size study score. 320pp. 8⅜ x 11¼. 23753-2

Haydn, Joseph, STRING QUARTETS, OPP. 20 and 33, COMPLETE. Complete reproductions of the 12 masterful quartets (six each) of Opp. 20 and 33—in the reliable Eulenburg edition. 272pp. 8⅜ x 11¼. 24852-6

Haydn, Joseph, STRING QUARTETS, OPP. 42, 50 and 54. Complete reproductions of Op. 42 in D Minor; Op. 50, Nos. 1–6 ("Prussian Quartets") and Op. 54, Nos. 1–3. Reliable Eulenburg edition. 224pp. 8⅜ x 11¼. 24262-5

Haydn, Joseph, TWELVE STRING QUARTETS. 12 often-performed works: Op. 55, Nos. 1–3 (including *Razor*); Op. 64, Nos. 1–6; Op. 71, Nos. 1–3. Definitive Eulenburg edition. 288pp. 8⅜ x 11¼. 23933-0

Kreisler, Fritz, CAPRICE VIENNOIS AND OTHER FAVORITE PIECES FOR VIOLIN AND PIANO: With Separate Violin Part, *Liebesfreud, Liebesleid, Schön Rosmarin, Sicilienne and Rigaudon,* more. 64pp. plus slip-in violin part. 9 x 12. (Available in U.S. only) 28489-1

Mendelssohn, Felix, COMPLETE CHAMBER MUSIC FOR STRINGS. All of Mendelssohn's chamber music: Octet, Two Quintets, Six Quartets, and Four Pieces for String Quartet. (Nothing with piano is included.) Complete works edition (1874–7). Study score. 283pp. 9⅜ x 12¼. 23679-X

Mozart, Wolfgang Amadeus, COMPLETE STRING QUARTETS. Breitkopf & Härtel edition. All 23 string quartets plus alternate slow movement to K.156. Study score. 277pp. 9⅜ x 12¼. 22372-8

Mozart, Wolfgang Amadeus, COMPLETE STRING QUINTETS, Wolfgang Amadeus Mozart. All the standard-instrumentation string quintets, plus String Quintet in C Minor, K.406; Quintet with Horn or Second Cello, K.407; and Clarinet Quintet, K.581. Breitkopf & Härtel edition. Study score. 181pp. 9⅜ x 12¼. 23603-X

Schoenberg, Arnold, CHAMBER SYMPHONY NO. 1 FOR 15 SOLO INSTRUMENTS, OP. 9. One of Schoenberg's most pleasing and accessible works, this 1906 piece concentrates all the elements of a symphony into a single movement. 160 pp. 8⅜ x 11. (Available in U.S. only) 41900-2

Schubert, Franz, COMPLETE CHAMBER MUSIC FOR PIANOFORTE AND STRINGS. Breitkopf & Härtel edition. *Trout,* Quartet in F Major, and trios for piano, violin, cello. Study score. 192pp. 9 x 12. 21527-X

Schubert, Franz, COMPLETE CHAMBER MUSIC FOR STRINGS. Reproduced from famous Breitkopf & Härtel edition: Quintet in C Major (1828), 15 quartets and two trios for violin(s), viola, and violincello. Study score. 348pp. 9 x 12. 21463-X

Schumann, Clara (ed.), CHAMBER MUSIC OF ROBERT SCHUMANN, Superb collection of three trios, four quartets, and piano quintet. Breitkopf & Härtel edition. 288pp. 9⅜ x 12¼. 24101-7

Tchaikovsky, Peter Ilyitch, PIANO TRIO IN A MINOR, OP. 50. Charming homage to pianist Nicholas Rubinstein. Distinctively Russian in character, with overtones of regional folk music and dance. Authoritative edition. 120pp. 8⅛ x 11. 42136-8

Tchaikovsky, Peter Ilyitch and Borodin, Alexander, COMPLETE STRING QUARTETS. Tchaikovsky's Quartets Nos. 1–3 and Borodin's Quartets Nos. 1 and 2, reproduced from authoritative editions. 240pp. 8⅜ x 11¼. 28333-X

Available from your music dealer or write for free Music Catalog to
Dover Publications, Inc., Dept. MUBI, 31 East 2nd Street, Mineola, NY 11501
Visit us online at www.doverpublications.com